Only a split second delay had separated the lightning flash and the thunderclap. Danielle knew what that meant—the bolt had struck very close by, probably in Mr. Wiggins's cow field next door. Maybe even closer. It could even have hit in the upper pasture, where the horses were grazing.

A chill shot through Danielle's heart.

The horses!

THE BLACK STALLION SERIES

BOOKS BY WALTER FARLEY

The Black Stallion
The Black Stallion Returns
Son of the Black Stallion
The Island Stallion
The Black Stallion and Satan
The Black Stallion's Blood Bay Colt
The Island Stallion's Fury
The Black Stallion's Filly
The Black Stallion Revolts
The Black Stallion's Sulky Colt
The Island Stallion Races
The Black Stallion's Courage
The Black Stallion Mystery
The Horse-Tamer
The Black Stallion and Flame
Man o' War
The Black Stallion Challenged!
The Black Stallion's Ghost
The Black Stallion and the Girl
The Black Stallion Legend
The Young Black Stallion (with Steven Farley)

BOOKS BY STEVEN FARLEY

The Black Stallion's Shadow
The Black Stallion's Steeplechaser

YOUNG BLACK STALLION

② A Horse Called **Raven**

Steven Farley

Random House New York

For Oliver

www.randomhouse.com/kids

Library of Congress Catalog Card Number: 98-066868
ISBN: 0-679-89142-0 (trade) — ISBN: 0-679-99142-5 (lib. bdg.)
RL: 4.5

Printed in the United States of America
10 9 8 7 6 5 4 3 2 1

Contents

1.	Storm!	1
2.	Magic Touch	11
3.	Picture-Perfect	21
4.	The Midnight Stallion	30
5.	Good-bye	39
6.	Dylan's Gold	44
7.	Treasure Hunt	51
8.	Horseshoe Head	59
9.	Another Try	68
10.	Changes	75
11.	The Weanling	83
12.	Waiting	93
13.	Vanished!	97
14.	Lulu's Hideaway	104
15.	Last Wish	110
16.	Secret in the Stars	121
17.	Team Raven	129

CHAPTER ONE

Storm!

Outside Danielle Conners's bedroom window, the Florida sun beat down on the pastures and paddocks of her family's farm. Twelve-year-old Danielle was sitting on the edge of her bed, thumbing through a pile of dollar bills stacked in front of her.

"Nine...ten...eleven," she counted aloud. "That makes a grand total of one hundred and twenty-two dollars."

She flopped back on the bed with a sigh. Ordinarily that would have seemed like a lot of money, but right now her goal of a thousand dollars was as far away as some pot of gold at the end of a rainbow.

Turning her head, she stared at the photograph in the little black frame on her nightstand. Redman's dark, searching eyes looked back at her. Her horse was a nine-year-old paint, red with big splotches of white, and a pure rusty-red mane and

1

tail. You couldn't see all of his markings in the close-up photo, just the spot masking his left eye that made him look like a pirate.

How will I ever get enough money together to buy Redman back? Danielle asked herself. At this rate, it could take forever. Her only income came from helping out with the two horses stabled in the barn behind her house. She'd been paid twice over the past month and she had barely saved a tenth of what she needed.

At least the job was fun. Prima and her foal, Little Buddy, belonged to Alec Ramsay. *The* Alec Ramsay, the handsome, mysterious young guy who rode the Black, just about the most famous race-horse ever. And Little Buddy had even been sired by the Black.

Danielle gathered the cash together and twisted a rubber band around the bills. Then she went over to her closet and carefully tucked the money into the pocket of her jacket. After pacing the floor a few times, she sat down on her bed again. Her thoughts, as usual, returned to Redman.

No matter how she put things together, she always ended up at the same place. Redman was a riding-camp horse now, way up in North Carolina. Her last hope of bringing him home was to buy him back from Mr. Sweet, Redman's new owner. Danielle had actually tried to do that already, with money she'd found (and later returned). But Mr. Sweet had hinted that he might sell Redman back to her *if* she earned the money herself. There could be no loans from generous relatives or anyone else—not that *that* was about to happen. Her family was in a tough spot over finances these days. Obviously, Mr. Sweet was trying to teach her a lesson about responsibility, and the value of money. *As if I don't understand that already,* Danielle thought miserably. *He's the rich guy, not me.*

Well, she reminded herself, she had no one to blame but herself. If she hadn't made Mr. Sweet so angry, maybe Redman wouldn't be slaving away at that riding camp up north right now.

Oh, stop it! Danielle thought. There was no use in kicking herself about it all over again. Her gaze returned to Redman's photo, then moved to the piece of paper lying beside it—the unfinished letter she was writing to Mr. Sweet. Like it or not, the fate of her horse lay in his hands. She picked up the letter and thought again about what she should say. She needed to choose her words carefully.

She took a deep breath. Somehow, some way, she was going to get Redman back—and soon. She loved Prima, and especially Little Buddy, but for her, no horse would ever be able to replace Redman. He was her best friend, the one who had always been there for her. Now the time had come for her to be there for Redman. She wasn't going to let him down.

Danielle reread the words she'd written. She needed to start again. With a groan, she rolled over onto her back and stared up at the ceiling. This was getting really depressing. She tossed the paper and pencil back on the nightstand and looked at her clock radio. It was one-thirty on a Sunday afternoon.

What am I doing moping around my room? she thought. Sure, she missed Redman, but thinking about him all the time was driving her nuts. It was better to keep busy. She needed to do something, anything, to get her mind off Redman and her desperate need for dollars.

Even though Alec had given her the day off, Danielle decided to head over to the barn and see what was up. There were always chores to do around the barn these days—tack to be cleaned, wraps to be washed, fences to be mended...

Fences. *Oops!* Hadn't she promised Alec that she would repair some loose rails in the lower pasture yesterday morning? She had forgotten completely about that.

Danielle quickly pulled on her work clothes: jeans and a blue flannel shirt. Glancing in the mirror, she pushed her blond bangs out of her eyes and pulled her shoulder-length hair back into a ponytail.

There was no sign of her mom as she stepped

into the kitchen to grab a can of soda from the refrigerator. Maybe she was at her desk in the studio upstairs. Dylan, Danielle's fourteen-year-old brother, was probably rummaging around in the tool shed or off visiting friends. Danielle tramped out onto the porch, banging the screen door behind her.

In the far pasture she could see the horses. Little Buddy was happily frolicking beside his Argentina-bred mother, Prima Gavilan. The foal spun around and kicked his heels to the sky. He was just five months old, so young that he didn't have an official name yet. Usually Alec and Danielle just called him "the colt" or "Little Buddy."

Danielle watched the prancing black colt and smiled. Handling a horse that age was a completely new experience for her. Redman and the other horses who used to be stabled at the farm were a lot older. For Danielle, taking care of Little Buddy this past month had been a lifesaver. Whenever she was feeling blue about losing Redman, it was the colt that usually managed to cheer her up.

Someday Little Buddy would train to become a racehorse like his father, the Black, but at this stage he was learning the same lessons any well-behaved horse had to know. Alec had told her that teaching the colt good manners now, like understanding what "whoa" meant and not fighting back against the lead line, would be very important for his later career. From watching the gentle way Alec handled the colt, Danielle was beginning to learn more about Alec, too. Usually, they talked about the horses and little else. But she didn't need to know the young jockey all that well to see how he felt about his own horse, the Black. Whenever he spoke about the stallion, he would smile and his eyes would shine. Danielle was sure Alec understood what it was like to love one horse above all others. That was the way she felt about Redman.

Danielle was surprised to see Alec's pickup parked in the driveway beside the guest cottage, where he was living. The Coop, as everyone called it, had been converted from a chicken coop into a cozy three-room apartment. Framed sketches of horses hung on the walls, and a window looked out over the barn and paddock.

Even on weekends, Alec didn't hang around the Coop much during the day. He divided most of his time between doing chores in the barn, running errands in town, and working at South Wind, the Thoroughbred training center a few miles away. It was there that the Black and some other horses from Hopeful Farm, Alec's home base in upstate New York, were being stabled for the winter.

Alec had hired Billy Spicer, a local horseman who liked to wear broad-brimmed cowboy hats and aviator sunglasses, as an assistant trainer. Billy often looked in on Prima and her foal when Alec and Danielle weren't around. Alec wanted to keep a close eye on the colt at this stage in the young horse's life. Little Buddy had all the makings of a good racehorse. With a bit of luck, he might even develop into a champion, like his sire, the Black.

Taking care of the colt and his mama certainly was a seven-day-a-week job, Danielle thought. Horses didn't take holidays or days off. They didn't care if it was Christmas, the Fourth of July, or somebody's birthday. They needed exercise, clean stalls, water, and feed.

And right now they need that fencing in the lower pasture fixed, Danielle told herself, feeling a bit guilty for having forgotten. She never would have taken the morning off if her mom hadn't dragged her to the mall to buy some new sneakers. Luckily, the horses had the whole upper pasture to play in. It was just a little farther away from the barn.

Danielle sipped her soda as she crossed the short distance from her house to the barn. She looked up to see dark clouds gathering in the western sky. *Rain,* she thought. The warm breeze carried a faint hint of the damp, earthy smell that often signaled an approaching cloudburst.

There was no sign of Alec inside the barn.

Danielle avoided looking in Redman's old stall. It was still painful for her to see it empty, a constant reminder that he was gone. Glancing into the tack room, she saw Redman's bridle hanging on a peg in the wall. Next to it was his saddle, which she kept clean and well-oiled in anticipation of his return.

Time to fix that fence, she reminded herself. She walked over to the tool alcove to look for a hammer.

Just then, Danielle heard the low rumbling sound of distant thunder. She stopped in her tracks and stood still, listening. "Uh-oh," she said aloud. A cool draft swept through the barn. She stepped over to the intercom that Alec had installed in the tack room, connecting the barn with his cottage and the Conners's house, and pushed the "talk" button. The intercom on the tack-room desk began to crackle.

"Alec?" Danielle called into the microphone. She smiled to herself. It was pretty cool being on a first-name basis with a world-famous jockey.

"Alec?" she called again, a little louder this time. No answer. She took a swig of soda and put the can back down on the desk. "Hey! Alec! Pick up."

"What is it, Danielle?" came Alec's voice over the tinny speaker. He sounded sleepy.

"Sorry to bother you, but have you looked outside recently? I think it might storm."

"Really?" Alec said. "The weather report said it's supposed to be sunny all weekend."

"Well, I heard thunder," Danielle said. "Shouldn't we bring the horses in from the pasture?"

"Okay," Alec said. "I'll be right there." The intercom clicked off.

Danielle poked her head outside the barn door. Clusters of dark clouds were racing across the sky. Somewhere, a loose shutter was banging on its hinges. Danielle went back to the tack room and grabbed a yellow rain slicker from the coat rack, just in case.

Alec was jogging over from the Coop. His red hair was mussed and his shirttail was only half tucked into his pants. The laces of one of his moccasins were untied. "I was catching up on some paperwork. Guess I dozed off. What time is it, anyway?"

Danielle checked her watch. "Getting on toward two."

Alec rubbed the back of his neck and gazed up at the ominous lead-colored clouds.

"It might just blow over," Danielle said. "Storms around here sometimes do."

Alec's expression turned serious. "I'd rather not take any chances. The last thing I need on my hands right now is a panicky colt."

Suddenly a brilliant silver-white light filled the room around them, like a thousand and one flashbulbs going off all at once.

Lightning! Danielle cringed and ducked her head.

The burst was punctuated immediately by a crack of thunder.

Tremors from the shock wave worked their way through the ground, causing the whole barn to rattle and shake. The soda can that Danielle had left on the table danced around, then teetered and fell to the floor.

Only a split-second delay had separated the lightning flash and the thunderclap. Danielle knew what that meant. The bolt had struck very close by, probably in Mr. Wiggins's cow field next door. Maybe even closer. It could even have hit in the upper pasture.

A chill shot through Danielle's heart.

The horses!

CHAPTER TWO

Magic Touch

Alec bolted for the door. "Stay here!" he shouted to Danielle over his shoulder. "I have to get the horses inside." He dashed out of the barn and vaulted the four-rail fence enclosing the pasture.

Another pitchfork of electricity blazed overhead and came crashing to earth out by the road. Danielle winced at the earthshaking thunderclap, then clenched her fists. *I can't just stand here doing nothing,* she told herself. Prima and Little Buddy were completely exposed to lightning in an empty field. It was just about the worst possible danger a horse could be in.

She sprinted out into the storm, almost tripping over her own feet as she ran. If the horses had been in the lower pasture, they would have been closer to the barn. Getting them inside would have been a lot easier, Danielle knew. *If only I'd fixed that stupid fence yesterday like I was supposed to!* she scolded herself.

Alec was probably thinking the same thing.

In a matter of seconds, the full force of the storm swept over. Rain spilled from the sky, lightning flashed, and wind howled. Static electricity charged the air around her. Danielle could feel the hair on the back of her neck standing up all on its own.

Prima and Little Buddy were huddling together under the tallest oak tree in the pasture. *Oh no!* Danielle thought. That was the worst possible place they could choose to wait out the storm. Trees were often the first things to be hit when lightning struck. The trembling colt was pressing up close to his mama, as if she could offer some sort of protection from the storm. His shrill whinnies filled the air.

Danielle heard Alec before she saw him. He was calling to the horses, trying to calm them. "Easy now, Prima! That's my girl. Come on now, Little Buddy. It'll all be okay." Both horses' ears were pinned back, and their legs were shaking. Their eyes were wide with fear, their nostrils flared.

Alec stepped in front of Prima. The mare's only reaction was the faintest nod. Alec reached out and put his hand on the mare's muzzle. Then he whisked on a halter and clipped on the lead line. Stepping back, he gave the line a gentle tug, but Prima was frozen with fear. She refused to budge.

Danielle looked at the colt, who continued to

shrill as he pushed closer to the mare. Both horses seemed convinced that the only safe place in the entire universe at that moment was under that tree.

Alec turned when he realized that Danielle was behind him. "What are you doing out here, Danielle?" he snapped. "Didn't you hear me tell you to stay in the barn? Prima and Little Buddy are my responsibility, not yours. It's dangerous out here."

"But it's my fault they're stuck way out here," Danielle shouted over the wind. "I'm the one who didn't fix that fencing and…"

"It's too late to worry about that now," Alec shouted back.

"But I can help! You might need me."

Alec was in no mood to argue. "Back me up, then. But whatever you do, don't get between me and them." Danielle nodded, and Alec turned his attention back to the horses.

Prima and Alec stared at each other. Danielle stood by on her tiptoes, ready to do whatever Alec told her. How would Alec break the standoff? she wondered. He was one slightly built guy against a ton of stubborn horseflesh.

"Come on, now, Prima," Alec soothed. "You don't want to stay out here in all this rain, do you?"

Alec began stroking Prima gently between the eyes. One of the mare's ears pricked forward, then the other. Instead of fighting the mare by continuing to pull on the line, Alec surprised Danielle by doing just the opposite. He pressed himself hard up against the horse, forcing her even closer to the tree.

The mare pushed back, only a few inches at first. Then, as Alec kept up the pressure, she heaved herself toward him. Alec gave way, and Prima suddenly staggered forward, away from the tree. Alec repeated the process, with the same result. Soon the two of them were jogging up the pasture path with the colt tagging close behind. Danielle ran beside them through the streaming rain. The safety of the barn seemed very far away.

Alec's singsong voice was a gentle, rhythmic chant above the howling wind and rain. "Easy now, guys...That's it...That's my angels..."

Suddenly, there was another flash of lightning and a crack of thunder. The colt bolted, spinning around and lunging away. Danielle dodged his charge and then chased after him. Catching up, she managed to get one hand on his neck. His coat felt like a handful of wet feathers.

"Whoa now, Little Buddy," she said. "That's far enough," The colt shook his head and snorted as she gently eased him around. Alec stopped to wait for them, and Prima called to her foal with a shrill whinny. A second later, the confused colt was running back to his mama as fast as his little hoofs could carry him.

Yet another flash of lightning split the sky, and the colt tried to squeeze in between Prima's legs. The mare swung her hips toward him, threatening to throw a hind hoof. Little Buddy reluctantly backed off a few inches. Alec patiently waited, then urged Prima on again, keeping just enough tension in the lead line to let the mare know that he was there. He gave the rope an extra wrap around his hand for a double grip and seemed ready to jump out of the way in case Prima bolted.

Danielle's heart raced as she jogged along beside Alec and the horses. She felt very vulnerable out in the middle of the pasture. Wind-driven swirls of rain were shooting from one direction and then another, stinging her face and hands like tremendous swarms of biting insects. But it was the lightning that really scared her. They were making very good targets of themselves by being out in the open like this.

Danielle swallowed, wondering if Alec knew that this part of Florida was famous as the "Lightning Capital of the World." Her parents had warned her and Dylan about it since they were little kids. Over the years, horses had been struck by lightning at Overton Farm and a number of other farms in the area.

Slowly but surely, the group jogged along toward the barn. When they finally reached the gate to the lower pasture, the horses slowed to a walk in single file. But as Prima neared the barn and saw her nice dry stall beckoning to her, she broke into a trot again. The colt stayed close at her heels. Alec escorted them both into the paddock. Danielle carefully closed the gate behind them and gave a huge sigh of relief. A moment later, they all were safely inside the shelter of the barn.

Alec removed Prima's lead line from her halter and clipped the mare to the cross-ties in the barn corridor. Then he filled a pail with warm water from the tap and gave the horses a couple sips. While Danielle held the colt, who was still jittery from all the excitement, Alec set to work with the scraper. He swept it over Prima's broad back to remove as much water from the mare's coat as he could.

"That's my guy," Danielle whispered reassuringly to Little Buddy, gently patting the colt's neck. "Everything's gonna be all right now."

She kept patting the colt and watched Alec work with silent admiration. The scene under the tree was still fresh in her mind.

"How'd you know Prima would react the way she did when you pushed her back?" she asked. "That was so cool. It was like magic."

Alec laughed. "No magic, Danielle. Just common sense. If I'd pulled on the lead line any harder, Prima would have just dug in her heels. Then I might never have been able to make her listen."

Danielle shook her head. "I didn't think there was any way you were going to get her to budge," she said.

"Henry Dailey showed me that trick once when we were trying to load a cranky old mare into a trailer," Alec explained. "He said it has to do with a horse's natural instinct to resist an aggressor."

Danielle nodded. She'd never met Henry Dailey, but she knew he was Hopeful Farm's head trainer back in New York. "You mean like trying to get what you want by asking for just the opposite? My mom calls that reverse psychology."

Alec chuckled. "Something like that."

The rain continued to fall. It sounded as if someone was pelting the barn roof with handfuls of gravel.

"Okay, Danielle," Alec said. "See if you can find some towels and give Prima a quick once-over. Just her back and neck. Nice and easy. Stay away from her legs. She's still a little jumpy, I think."

Alec set to work on Little Buddy while Danielle led Prima to the large stall she shared with the colt. Danielle spoke softly to the mare as she worked some of the dampness out of Prima's coat with a towel.

When she had finished, Danielle stepped back to admire her work. Prima had calmed down a lot, and the mare looked beautiful. She was a dark bay color with darker legs and a black mane and tail. Her chest was deep, her hocks and shoulders high. She was lean, despite her recent motherhood, with a long back and good hindquarters. There was a proud, self-confident air to her, as if she was aware of her good looks and glad that they pleased her handlers. Tossing her head, the mare pawed the ground restlessly.

"Shush now, pretty mama," Danielle said. She peeked over the door to watch Alec rubbing out the colt. Little Buddy's coat was even darker than Prima's. That made sense, since he had been sired by the Black. At five months, he had a fine, delicate head, long spindly legs, and straight knees. His eyes were large and fired with excitement. The shape and placement of the white star on his forehead, identical to his dam's, marked him as Prima's foal.

But, Danielle knew, Little Buddy was the Black's colt, too. That meant people would be expecting a lot of him. As she watched Alec work, she had to remind herself that, though Alec plainly loved Prima and Little Buddy, to him they weren't just beautiful horses. They were a vital part of his business. With luck, the colt would be a champion someday. That meant a lot of pressure for Alec because, at the moment, Little Buddy was all his responsibility.

Sure, Danielle thought, Alec was a pro. He was a successful jockey and all-around horseman. But he was still only eighteen years old. It couldn't be easy to live with so much responsibility and the constant pressure to win. In a funny way, she almost felt sorry for Alec sometimes.

Danielle glanced out the window. The dark clouds in the sky were already giving way to patches of blue. "Looks like the storm's blowing over fast, just like it came in," she said.

"Good," Alec replied, sounding tired. "We'll move the horses out again as soon as the rain stops. I don't like to keep a colt like Little Buddy inside any more than I have to."

A few minutes later, the last of the clouds swept eastward. Alec led the horses out of the barn and into the glistening sunlight. Water droplets sparkled on the leaves of the trees. "Fresh air and sunshine is the best thing for these guys right now," Alec said.

He and Danielle turned Prima and Buddy loose in the paddock. A distant rumble of thunder sent the little black colt pressing up close to Prima again, but he seemed smart enough to realize quickly that the danger was past. Before long, he began running around on his own. He zigzagged about the paddock, whirling like a top.

Prima moved sweetly along the length of the

paddock, flicking her tail in the sunlight. Danielle's mom, who had been around horses all her life, had said that Prima was one of the finest-looking mares she had ever seen. Danielle had to agree.

The faint sound of a banging screen door made Danielle turn. Her mom was waving to her from the porch steps. Danielle ran across the yard and driveway toward her.

"Danielle!" Mrs. Conners said, sounding a little worried. "What in the world have you been up to? Where have you been?"

"Um...nowhere, Mom," Danielle said.

Mrs. Conners tapped her foot on the steps and eyed her daughter suspiciously. "What were you doing out in that storm, young lady? Are you trying to give me a heart attack? I thought you were still in your room. Get in here and put on some dry clothes."

"Yes, Mom," Danielle said meekly.

"But first go tell Alec that Henry Dailey called. He wants Alec to call him back right away. It's important. Something about a horse race in California."

CHAPTER THREE

Picture-Perfect

Danielle ran to the paddock, where Alec was leaning on a fence rail watching Little Buddy, and gave him Henry's message.

Alec hurried off. His face had seemed to tighten, whether from excitement or anxiety Danielle couldn't tell. She glanced at Little Buddy, who was splashing around in a mud puddle, then reluctantly headed back to the house. Her mom caught her at the kitchen door.

"You look like a drowned rat, Danielle," Mrs. Conners said as she followed her daughter into the house. "And please don't tell me those are the new sneakers I just bought you. Look at that mud!"

Danielle glanced down at her feet and cringed. It was true. She had forgotten to change them when she came home from town this afternoon. "Oops," she said. "Sorry."

Mrs. Conners threw up her hands. "Give me a break, Danielle. Your father and I worked hard for the money to buy those shoes."

"I know, I know," Danielle said. She took her shoes off and left them on the porch by the front door. Two at a time, she climbed the stairs to her room to change into a dry shirt, pants, and her old sneakers. Then she came back downstairs and set to work cleaning the mud stains off her new Nikes with a rag.

Her mom was talking on the phone and hung up as Danielle came into the kitchen. Danielle broke into a breathless description of how Alec had handled the horses caught out in the pasture.

Mrs. Conners gave her daughter a preoccupied smile as she fumbled through her purse. "Mmm. That's nice, dear. Have you seen that brother of yours? He's supposed to be helping me with something."

"He's probably over at Dave's house," Danielle said. She looked impatiently toward the door. "I have to get back to the barn, Mom. There's a chore I have to do."

"Okay, then," said Mrs. Conners. "But before you go back outside or anywhere else, I want those wet clothes in the wash room."

"Sure, Mom."

Danielle did as she was told and then went back

outside to patch the fence in the lower pasture. Alec hadn't mentioned it, but Danielle didn't want him to think she was irresponsible. Knocking the rails together to fix the fence didn't take long at all.

As she returned the hammer to the tool alcove in the barn, she heard someone calling her name. She went outside to find Julie Burke pedaling up the driveway on her bike. Julie was Danielle's best friend and number-one riding partner. Or used to be, when Redman had been around. Between them, they knew practically every trail and back road in the whole county. They were in the same class at Wishing Wells Middle School, so they saw each other every day.

Julie coasted to a stop next to Danielle and hopped off her bike. A camera was hanging from her neck.

Danielle and Julie slapped palms. "Hey, where'd you get the camera?" Danielle asked.

"My uncle Tim sent it to me. Sort of a late birthday present. It's one of his old ones. Pretty nice, huh?"

Danielle took the camera in her hands. It felt solid and heavy. "Cool."

"I was out taking pictures on my bike when the storm hit," Julie went on. "I just made it to Shootzy's Diner in time for cover. I don't think this camera is waterproof. I sure hope I didn't wreck the thing."

Danielle held the camera up to her face and

peered through the viewfinder. "Any film left in it?"

"Sure." Julie struck a pose, pretending to be a fashion model, and fluffed her short, wavy dark hair.

"You look absolutely fabulous, dah-ling," Danielle told her, grinning.

"Hey, let's take some pictures of the horses," Julie said. "Do you think Alec would mind?"

Danielle shook her head. "Nah, but we should probably ask him, anyway."

The girls headed to the barn to look for Alec. They found him in the tack room, going over some business papers he must have brought from the Coop.

"Good afternoon, ladies," Alec said, looking up from his work and smiling at Julie.

Julie gave Alec a little wave and shuffled her feet self-consciously. "Uh, hi," she said softly. Once again, Danielle noticed the effect Alec's presence seemed to have on her usually level-headed friend. The same thing had happened the last time Julie came over. Danielle frowned. She was beginning to suspect Julie was developing a hopeless crush on Alec.

"Nice camera," Alec said.

"Thanks," Julie said brightly. "It's new. I mean, old."

Danielle elbowed her friend.

"Um...oh, Alec," Julie said, "I was just wondering...would it be okay for me to take some pictures of Prima and Little Buddy?"

"Sure, go ahead," Alec said, looking down at his work again. "Knock yourself out. They're both pretty well calmed down now."

As they left the barn, Julie glanced back at the handsome young jockey. "Come on," Danielle said disgustedly. "Let's go."

The two of them climbed through the paddock fence and walked over to Prima and Little Buddy. Danielle rubbed the colt's neck and let him nuzzle the side of her face. Julie reached up and gave the mare a pat on the neck.

"Okay," Julie said. "Let's get busy." She began shooting the horses from different angles, clicking away with the camera. The colt seemed to like having his picture taken. If Danielle hadn't known better, she would have sworn he was hamming it up for the camera, playing in puddles and hopping around like crazy.

Danielle leaned against a fence post and watched her friend. Julie loved movies. She even talked about wanting to be a film director someday.

A few minutes later, Alec joined them at the paddock fence. Julie looked up from her camera's viewfinder. "I sure would like to take pictures of the Black someday," she said. "I've seen him on TV and all, but has he ever been in a movie?"

Alec didn't answer right away. He just stood

there, fidgeting with two lengths of rope he was braiding together. "We shot a commercial out in California once," he said finally. "It wasn't a very big part, but that was fine with me."

"What was it for?" asked Danielle.

"Oh, it wasn't really a commercial. It was a public service announcement for the ASPCA."

"I don't think they ever showed it down here," Danielle said.

"Doesn't surprise me," Alec said with a shrug. "I only saw it once or twice myself." He draped the strands of rope over the fence rail. "The Black isn't much for standing around and posing for pictures. That's not his style. He's had one heck of a life. He was born in the Arabian desert, you know. And years ago he saved my life during a shipwreck, just for starters."

"Wow," Julie said. She was staring at Alec, hanging on to every word with wide-eyed fascination.

"What's your favorite movie, Alec?" Danielle asked.

Alec thought for a minute.

"Favorite movie? Hmm—Let's see…The last one I really liked was some film about Australian cowboys. Right now, I can't even remember the name." He scratched his chin. "I think it was *The Last Cowboy* or *The Lost Cowboy* or something like that."

"I bet Mr. Lyman would know," Julie said. "He's

probably seen every movie ever made. He's always talking about them."

Danielle nodded in agreement. "You'd like Mr. Lyman, Alec. He was our substitute teacher the week before last, when Mrs. Currie was sick. He's from up north, like you. He'd been all over the world and done all sorts of work."

"Sounds great," Alec said, coiling up the strands of rope again.

Danielle shook her head. "Yeah, but he was really different. I mean, we actually looked *forward* to going to Mr. Lyman's class in the morning, didn't we, Julie?"

Julie nodded. "Yeah, he was cool."

Alec smiled. "I would have liked to meet him."

"I think he went back up north," Danielle said. "That's what Mrs. Currie told us, anyway."

"It seems like everyone leaves Wishing Wells if they can," Julie said. "There aren't a whole lot of job opportunities around here."

Danielle glanced at Alec. If it weren't for his stabling his horses at the farm, her family probably wouldn't be staying, either. Her dad was on the road a lot as a struggling country singer, and her mom's freelance design jobs didn't pay much.

"Well, *I* like Wishing Wells," said Alec with a grin.

"You'll probably change your mind before long," Julie said.

Alec laughed and gave her a friendly rap on the head with his knuckles. "You two girls are screwy. Why don't you kick the soccer ball around with the colt awhile?"

"Want to, Julie?" Danielle asked her friend.

"Sure," Julie said. "Hey, maybe we can get a picture of Little Buddy kicking the ball. You never know, I might even be able to sell the picture to the newspaper. It's not every day people see a soccer-playing horse."

"Go ahead. Give it a shot." Alec picked up the soccer ball that was under the bench beside the barn door and rolled it to Danielle. "Hey, Alec," Danielle said. "Did you remember to phone Henry?"

"Yeah, I did. Thanks. No one answered, so I'll try again later. He's out in California with a couple of our horses. I sure hope everything is all right." Alec sounded a little nervous.

Danielle turned away, reminded once again how serious the horse business was to someone like Alec. She wondered if Little Buddy had the slightest idea of what was in store for him in the years to come.

She began to knock the soccer ball around the paddock with the colt. Julie took pictures of them chasing the ball together.

Julie laughed as Little Buddy gave the ball a smack with his hind legs and sent it sailing out of the paddock. "Your turn," Julie called to Danielle. Giving the colt a dirty look, Danielle hopped the fence and ran after the ball.

"Where did you ever get this crazy idea anyway?" Julie asked Alec, who came up as Danielle returned with the ball.

"It was really Danielle's idea," Alec said.

Danielle nodded. "I was kicking the ball in the driveway one afternoon about a week ago," she explained. "It got away from me and landed in the paddock. The colt started dancing around, kicking and chasing it."

"All on his own?" asked Julie.

Alec smiled. "That's right. I saw the way the colt was reacting, and the next day I bought a ball for him. From then on, soccer has been part of Little Buddy's daily routine. I think it's helping to develop his reflexes."

"And it's fun—if you don't mind chasing after a ball all afternoon," Danielle added. "Little Buddy's not much of a team player."

"Only you could get a job playing soccer with a horse, Danielle," Julie said. "Maybe we can get him to join the team at school."

They all watched as the colt gave the ball a few taps and then punted it out of the paddock again.

Danielle grinned. Little Buddy was really catching on.

"Your turn!" she called to Julie.

The Midnight Stallion

"Okay, Danielle," Alec said after Julie had left for home. "Playtime's over. Want to show me how you and Little Buddy are getting on with the lead line?"

"Sure," Danielle said. She went to the tack room and brought out the new web halter and lead shank she and Alec had bought in town.

Even though the halter and lead were nothing new to the colt—he'd been acquainted with them for over a month now—they were still a big part of his daily routine. Alec's way of training a horse relied on constant repetition and patience. He didn't "break" his horses, the way some trainers did. He "gentled" them.

Danielle slipped the halter over Little Buddy's head and buckled it, then ran her hands behind his small ears, finding the spots she knew he enjoyed being rubbed. "Good boy. Good Little Buddy," she said as she clipped the lead line to the halter rings. "Are you feeling all better now?" She moved with the colt as he walked along, letting the line swing loosely between them.

"Good work, Danielle," Alec called. "Keep the line slack. Remember, we're not trying to control him—just getting him used to the lead. Teaching him to respond to signals from us takes time."

Danielle nodded. Alec had been saying the same thing for weeks. *When are we going on to the next stage?* she wondered.

They moved Little Buddy's lesson outside the paddock. For the next half hour, Danielle let the colt lead her around the lower pasture. After a while, Alec clipped a lead line to Prima's halter and brought her out to the pasture, too. Prima whinnied for her colt, but Little Buddy seemed so busy nosing around that he barely paid any attention.

"Let him have his own way if he wants," Alec said.

As the colt's walk changed to a trot, Danielle quickened her own pace. Despite Little Buddy's sudden spurts of speed, Danielle managed to stay near enough that the line never became taut. Fortunately, the colt wasn't running his fastest or straying too far from the mare. On and on through the pasture they went, Danielle beside them, able to stay with the horses as long as she kept on her toes.

Little Buddy circled his mother, curiously eyeing the line stretched between him and Danielle. Finally, he stopped and remained standing close beside

Prima. Danielle stood still and waited, talking gently to him.

"Okay," Alec called, "now let's try a little restraint." He told Danielle to lead the colt away and back again. This time, when the colt came to a stop beside Prima, Alec led the mare away from him. Little Buddy tugged playfully on the line and whinnied, but Danielle firmly held her ground.

"Easy, guy," Danielle said. "Wait just a second now. That's it."

Still talking softly to the colt, she kept holding on to the line to prevent him from following his mother. After a few moments, Alec gave her the signal to let Little Buddy move slowly toward the mare. At first, the colt tried to break away from Danielle and run to Prima, but Danielle carefully held him to a walk.

"Good going," Alec said. "Real good. He's getting better every time."

Next, Danielle guided the colt to the fence and tied the end of the line to a post.

Little Buddy bobbed his head a few times but otherwise stood still, calm and relaxed. "Terrific," Alec said, smiling proudly. "No fuss at all today."

Danielle nodded, but it was hard to see why this was any big deal.

"I know it doesn't seem like much," Alec said, reading her mind, "but learning to stand tied without fighting the rope is very important for Buddy at this stage of the game. A horse that can't stand tied by himself without getting into trouble isn't much good to anyone."

They turned Prima and Little Buddy loose again, then took them back to the barn just before sunset. Alec was in the middle of telling Danielle about the next day's training schedule when Mrs. Conners buzzed the intercom to ask Alec to join the family for dinner. He thanked her but declined. Danielle didn't know why. It probably wasn't her mom's cooking, which was usually pretty good. She guessed he was probably just a little shy. Though he always acted friendly with everyone, Alec seemed to enjoy his privacy.

Danielle's mom stepped onto the porch to clang the dinner bell. "See you later," Danielle called to Alec, heading toward the house. She could smell the steak, potatoes, and broccoli her mother was dishing up in the kitchen.

Dylan followed her a minute later. He'd been out in the tool shed, pulling apart a box stapler he'd found somewhere. Her brother loved mechanical things. He spent hours tearing them up and hunting odd-looking gears and sprockets. The tool shed was constantly cluttered with butchered-up sewing machines, antique adding machines, old radios, telephones, and other junk. Even though he'd given a lot of his treasures away to his friends last month when the family had been planning a move to the coast, the stuff had already started piling up again.

"I heard from your father this afternoon," Mrs. Conners said, as the three of them sat down at the table.

"Really?" Danielle asked eagerly. She always missed her dad when he was away on tour with his band.

"He's still in Texas," Mrs. Conners said. "I think he—"

"So when's he coming home?" Danielle interrupted.

"Not for another couple weeks, honey. To tell you the truth, we'll be lucky to get him home for Christmas. You know how busy the band gets during the holidays." She stopped suddenly and gave Dylan a critical glance as he wolfed down his food. "One mouthful at a time, Dylan. *Chew* your food."

"I gotta go," Dylan said, his mouth full. "I'm supposed to meet Dave at Shootzy's."

His mother shook her head. "That will just have to wait. We're having a family dinner here. You've had all day to play around."

"Playing? I've been working," Dylan protested.

Mrs. Conners raised her eyebrows. "Working, huh? So when was the last time you cleaned out your ferrets' cage?" she asked. "The tool shed is starting to smell."

"Okay, okay. I'll do it before I go," Dylan said.

"*And* tomorrow is a school day," Mrs. Conners went on. "That means homework tonight. Speaking of which..." She shifted her gaze between Danielle and Dylan.

Danielle stood up from the table. "I'm pretty well caught up on my homework, Mom. Excuse me, please. I have to get back to the barn."

Mrs. Conners put down her fork. "Whoa there, young lady."

Oh boy, thought Danielle, *here it comes.* She'd almost escaped.

"Don't you have some big report for English class this term?"

"Well, yeah." Danielle said.

"And?"

"Well, I had this great idea that would have been fun to write about for a change. But Mrs. Currie wouldn't approve the subject."

Mrs. Conners frowned. "That doesn't sound like Mrs. Currie. I always thought she was pretty open-minded." Mrs. Currie was so old that Danielle's mom had had her as a teacher when *she* was in school.

"I think she's just jealous," Danielle said. "Remember when I told you about Mr. Lyman, that cool substitute teacher we had?"

Mrs. Conners spooned another serving of broccoli onto Dylan's plate. "How could I forget? For a while there you could hardly start a sentence without 'Mr. Lyman says...'"

"Well, he gave me this great idea for my research paper, but Mrs. Currie said no. She thinks everything we did with Mr. Lyman was a waste of time."

"So what exactly makes this Mr. Lyman so great, then?" asked Danielle's mom. "I never really understood."

"Well, for one thing, he took the whole class outside one day and we sat in the grass under that big oak tree beside the playground. Then he told us this really amazing story."

Dylan was playing around with the leftover food on his plate. "That guy was weird."

"Shut up, Dylan," Danielle said. "Besides, you know you liked him, too. You told me so."

Mrs. Conners held up her hands. "Enough, you two. No fighting."

Danielle kept talking. "So you could tell he really loved telling us this story. He totally got into the characters, acting them out with different accents and voices. It was almost like watching a play."

Mrs. Conners began to collect the empty plates from the table and stack them. She gestured toward the sink. "Come on and help with the dishes. You too, Dylan." They all set to work cleaning up the kitchen. "I still don't see what this has to do with your homework," said Mrs. Conners.

Danielle picked up a dish towel. "I'm getting to that."

Her mother looked a little exasperated. "No twenty-minute excuses, Danielle. Please."

"So anyway, Mr. Lyman told us this story about Merkain," Danielle went on. "A.k.a. the Midnight Stallion."

Mrs. Conners looked confused. "Merkain, Mom," Danielle said. "Haven't you ever heard about him? Your great-grandparents were Irish, weren't they? Merkain is a magical flying horse. He's the spirit guardian of the King of Ireland's royal stable."

Danielle's mom splashed water over the dishes. "I see."

"Hey, what's next, D?" her brother said. "You gonna do a term paper on unicorns?"

Danielle ignored him. "Over in Ireland, lots of people believe in Merkain, Mr. Lyman says. They write songs and poems about him. I wrote one, too. Mr. Lyman said I should send it in to the yearbook. Want to hear?"

"Oh, please." Dylan rolled his eyes as Danielle cleared her throat.

"The Midnight Stallion roams the night,
Staying hidden, out of sight,
His powerful hoofs press the ground,
Then fly upward with a bound.

When he sees the morning light,
He disappears with the night."

Danielle's mom gave her a warm smile. "That's sweet, dear." Dylan snickered. "Be nice, young man," Mrs. Conners scolded.

"The scary thing is, nobody who rides the Midnight Stallion can ever get off," Danielle continued. "People just ride until they die. Or else Merkain flies down into the water and they drown. Something like that."

Dylan couldn't contain himself any longer. "That's the dumbest thing I ever heard!" he hooted.

Mrs. Conners gave him a warning look.

"Anyway, I wanted to do my report on Merkain and compare him to Pegasus, a Greek mythical horse, but Mrs. Currie said it wasn't part of the lesson plan."

"Well, then," her mother asked, "what *did* you finally decide to write about?"

"The history of the Florida pioneers. Mrs. Curry assigned it." Danielle sighed. "Merkain would have been a lot more exciting."

She closed her eyes a moment, imagining she was riding Redman across a green meadow. Only, Redman had wings, and he was lifting her up and away, above the clouds, higher and…

Dylan laughed, snapping Danielle out of her daydream. "Flying horses? Get real, Danielle."

ༀ CHAPTER FIVE ༀ

Good-bye

Before school the next morning, Danielle took a quick shower and ran to the barn. She went straight to work mucking out stalls, trying to save as much clean straw as possible, the way Alec had shown her. She finished and looked at her watch. Seven-thirty. She had five minutes to clean up and ten minutes for the bike ride to the bus stop at Shootzy's. So far, despite her tight schedule, she hadn't missed the bus yet.

Just then a red pickup rumbled into the drive-way. A few moments later, Alec walked into the barn. "The place looks good," he said, glancing around. "You've been doing a great job, Danielle."

Danielle smiled. It was nice to be appreciated, and this job sure made her feel needed. It also helped keep her mind off Redman. But the uncomfortable expression that suddenly came over Alec's

39

face told Danielle he had more on his mind right now than a tidy barn.

"Something's come up, Danielle," Alec said. "Something good in the long term, but it may not seem so good to you in the short term."

Danielle swallowed. She didn't like the sound of this.

"Remember that phone call from Henry yesterday? Well, I finally got in touch with him last night. One of our two-year-olds, Black Falcon, just won a race out in California. He even set a new track record for the event. And he's Little Buddy's brother."

"Brother?" Danielle echoed.

"That's right. Buddy is Prima's second foal. Black Falcon, her first, also was sired by the Black."

"Great." Danielle's heart lightened a bit. How could anything bad come out of Little Buddy's big brother winning a race? "I guess that means Buddy will be a winner someday, too."

Alec shrugged. "That would be nice. You never know quite what to expect with horses, though. Physical conformation and temperaments can vary a great deal from one offspring to another, just like they do in children with the same mother and father. But sure, we can't help but get our hopes up." He hesitated. "But now the spotlight is really going to be on Little Buddy. Henry thinks we should move him and Prima back to South Wind, at least for the time being."

Danielle's jaw dropped. *This can't be happening,* she thought. Last month she'd lost Redman. Was she going to lose Prima and Little Buddy now, too?

Alec nodded. "I know it's kind of sudden, Danielle, but Henry calls the shots. He thinks that Little Buddy will get better care with the other horses at South Wind."

Danielle couldn't believe her ears. South Wind was a horse farm only a couple of miles away, but it was still far enough that there was no way she could get there on her own.

"But how can you guys be so sure Little Buddy will be better off at South Wind?" Danielle asked.

"We can't. But Henry says we might end up doing the colt more harm than good by keeping him here. Henry's going to be splitting his time between California and New York, so Little Buddy is entirely in my hands. I need to play it safe."

"But he's safe *here,*" Danielle said.

Alec lowered his eyes. He seemed almost embarrassed. "I guess I made a mistake telling Henry about the horses getting caught in that storm yesterday."

"That could have happened anywhere, even at South Wind," Danielle protested.

"Yeah, I suppose so." Alec smiled sympathetically. "Just the same, Henry thinks the colt has too much potential for me to be experimenting with things like soccer and extra playtime. He wants to stick with more traditional training methods."

Danielle's chin dropped down to her chest. *This is all my fault,* she told herself. *I started Buddy playing around with that stupid soccer ball. I was the one who forgot to fix that fence so the horses were caught in the Upper Pasture during the storm. And now Alec is taking the blame.* "I'm sorry, Alec," she said finally. "It's all my fault."

"Don't be silly, Danielle," Alec said. "Personally, I think we're on the right track with Little Buddy. But Henry is an old-school type of trainer. I should have known he wouldn't buy the idea of a future champion racehorse playing tag and chasing soccer balls."

Danielle took a deep breath. She couldn't give up yet. "I still don't see why..." she began.

Alec held up his hands to cut her off. "It'll be better this way, Danielle. If we have an accident, or if anything else goes wrong, they have the facilities at South Wind to take care of the problem right away. The colt will have twenty-four-hour care, seven days a week."

"But Little Buddy gets plenty of attention here! Billy or you or I are always around the barn."

"*Almost* always," Alec reminded her. "You have to admit there are holes in the schedule sometimes."

Danielle stared at her feet. She felt completely defeated.

"Come on, Danielle. We're talking business here. These aren't pleasure horses on some rich guy's estate."

Danielle sighed. "Alec. I didn't mean to sound ungrateful. I was just starting to get used to things around here, that's all. And Little Buddy likes me. I like him, too."

Alec nodded. "You've both learned a lot in the past month, like I said. You should be proud. So don't worry. I'm going to be staying on in the Coop, and I'll bring some new horses here soon. In the meantime, I'm sure you can find another job. Come on, chin up." He glanced at his watch. "Don't you have to get to the bus?"

"Right," Danielle said hiding her face and the tears welling up in her eyes. By now she'd missed the bus for sure.

I'm really going to miss Little Buddy, she thought as she started back to the house. She'd miss the way he nuzzled her neck, and their endless games.

First Redman, now Little Buddy. It was hard to keep saying good-bye.

CHAPTER SIX

Dylan's Gold

In English class, Danielle's gaze wandered out the window, where the groundskeeper, Mr. Zivic, was raking leaves under a tree. There was no point in being angry at Alec, she decided finally. The orders to move Prima and Little Buddy had come from Henry Dailey, not Alec. And there were other jobs out there. She could find something. She *had* to. She'd promised Redman.

Baby-sitting, maybe. The problem with that was transportation. Most of the jobs were at night, and her mom definitely didn't like her roaming around the streets after dark. She'd learned that the hard way last month, when she'd snuck out to Mr. Sweet's ranch in Albritton. Once in a while, her mom might drive her, but Danielle doubted if she could talk her into doing it regularly.

"Ms. Conners?" Danielle snapped to attention. "Eyes front," Mrs. Currie said. "I'm sure the class

44

would like to have a status report on your project. Would you be so kind as to tell us how your research is progressing?"

Danielle blinked a few times. "My, uh, research?"

Laughter rippled through the classroom. Danielle felt her face grow hot.

Mrs. Currie nodded. She stared at Danielle from behind her thick round glasses, drumming her fingers on the desktop the way she always did when she'd caught one of her students goofing off. Finally, she sighed. "Try to pay attention, please, Danielle."

"Yes, ma'am," Danielle said.

"Good. Now then, about your research…"

"Well, my mom has a few books on Indians that I've been reading. And then there's the library…" In truth Danielle hadn't set foot inside a library in months. She'd promised herself she was going to go later today. Or maybe tomorrow.

"And what is your subject again?"

"Pioneer days in Florida, ma'am."

"Wonderful." *It should be,* Danielle told the teacher silently. *It was your idea.* "Now if you would please cut down on the cloud research out the window." With that, Mrs. Currie mercifully turned her attention on someone else. "Mr. Mead…" Danielle breathed a sigh of relief.

That noon, Danielle ate a lunch of macaroni

and cheese with Julie and their friend Teri. Like Julie, Teri was pretty in a cowgirl sort of way, except Teri's hair was darker and shorter and her eyes were a sparkling blue. She rode a six-year-old Morgan named Scooter. His name was sort of a joke, since Scooter was a big monster of a horse who did anything but scoot. Danielle figured they must have given it to him when he was very little. That made her think of Little Buddy and wonder if the same thing was going to happen to him. Pretty soon he would be getting much too big to be called "Little" anything.

Both Teri and Julie were sympathetic when Danielle told them her story, in between forkfuls of macaroni and swallows of grape juice. "We'll help you figure something out, Danielle," Julie said.

But Danielle knew everyone had her own problems. Teri was about to flunk math, and her parents had cut off her riding privileges. Julie had spent all of her allowance on film for her new camera. She hadn't realized that it didn't have automatic rewind, and she'd already wasted a whole roll of film by accidentally opening the back of the camera without winding up the film first.

When Danielle arrived home after school, the pastures and paddocks were empty. So were the stalls. There were no horses at all. Just quiet. It reminded her of a ghost town in an old Western movie. She half expected to see a tumbleweed roll by.

She stooped to pluck a blade of grass and stuck it between her teeth, feeling like a cow. She knew she should get started on her research paper, but somehow she couldn't get motivated to go inside and do it. She thought about calling Julie but changed her mind about that, too.

A jet passed overhead, and the sound made Danielle sort of sad. Soon it would be hundreds of miles away, and she would still be here, just chewing on grass. She wondered what Redman was doing right now.

Fifteen minutes later, the only thing that had changed was that the blade of grass in Danielle's mouth had been replaced by a wad of bubble gum. Now she was amusing herself by blowing bigger and bigger bubbles.

She walked over to the pasture fence. It would have been nice if Alec had waited for her to get home before he took the horses away. It sort of made her mad that he hadn't. At least she could have had a chance to say good-bye. What was the big hurry, anyway?

Her gaze followed the fence rails. For a moment she thought she saw Little Buddy and the mare racing along the fence at the far end of the pasture. But it was just a couple of shadows. Empty pastures. Empty paddocks. Empty barn. Empty stalls. Danielle sighed. *Empty me.*

Over the next few days, Danielle checked the bulletin boards at Shootzy's, the grocery store, and a few other places in town, looking for baby-sitting jobs. Out of five promising leads, two wanted someone older and two had already been filled. The last job was only for one night—this Saturday—but at least it was work.

The family lived on the other side of town, but Danielle's mom said she'd drive her. The kid turned out to be a really sweet eight-year-old boy named Randy, who spent most of the night playing video games. His regular baby-sitter was sick and Randy's parents promised to call her whenever the other girl couldn't make it. Still, Danielle knew she had to find a job for after school, or at least something a little more definite.

She kept checking bulletin boards and want ads in the newspaper, but the few ads she answered didn't work out. Either the job was too far away or they wanted someone older or the job required longer hours than Danielle's mother would allow. Juggling schoolwork with a job had been tricky enough when the job was in her own backyard. As hard as she tried, she just couldn't seem to find anything right.

The emptiness at the farm was almost unbearable. Alec came and went from the Coop with hardly a word, though he told Danielle that Prima and Little Buddy were settling in at South Wind.

Without Little Buddy around to distract her, Danielle was really starting to miss Redman again, too. She found an old videotape her dad had made once when they all went on a trail ride together and played the part with Redman in it over and over again. Sometimes it only made her feel worse, but she couldn't resist watching it. Every once in a while, Danielle snuck out to the tack room and buried her face in Redman's unwashed saddle blanket, just to remember what he smelled like.

One afternoon, Danielle was sitting on the back porch, feeling miserable, when Dylan came outside, a new CD player strapped to his belt. "Where'd you get that?" Danielle asked. Her brother was doing a little dance to the music with his eyes closed, so she had to tug on his arm to get his attention.

"Huh?" he said, startled.

"The CD player, Dylan. Who gave you that?"

Dylan shrugged. "No one. I bought it."

"*Bought* it?!" Danielle's mouth dropped open. Neither she nor her brother had been getting an allowance lately. "That must have cost a hundred bucks at least."

"One hundred nineteen to be exact," Dylan corrected. He whipped the player off his belt and pointed to some flashing gauges. "Look, it even has auto-tracking."

"So, where'd you get the money?" Danielle pressed.

"I've been saving it," Dylan said.

Danielle frowned. "From what? You don't have a job."

"Not exactly, but I do know where to pick up some change if I need to."

"How?" Danielle asked suspiciously.

Dylan grinned. "Come on, I'll show you." Danielle followed him around to the side of the tool shed, where he pointed to a heavy-duty garbage bag. Danielle looked inside and saw that it was filled with empty bottles and cans.

Dylan looked smug. "It's gold, little sister. Glass and aluminum gold."

Treasure Hunt

"What are you talking about, Dylan?" asked Danielle. She gave the garbage bag a nudge with her toe. "What is all this junk?"

"It's *not* junk," Dylan corrected. "It's money. Twenty of these equal one dollar!"

Danielle wrinkled up her nose. "They sure do stink. Rancid old soda cans. Yuck."

Dylan shrugged. "I used to wash them out, but it takes too much time. It's better just to cash them in as fast as you can."

"Does Mom know about this?"

"Sure. It's okay with her as long as I keep my work clothes out here and wash up as soon as I come in the house. So I need to take this load to the refund center at the Quick Stop. Want to give me a hand? I'll cut you in for a couple of bucks."

Danielle glanced back at her brother. *How could*

he sink so low? she asked herself. Dylan didn't seem to care. He began fiddling with the control knobs on his new CD player, and the faint *boom, boom, boom* of the bass and drums through the headset grew louder.

He nodded to the sack full of empty cans. "Well, what do you say?" he practically shouted over the music. Danielle gestured for her brother to take off his headphones.

"Aren't you embarrassed? What if someone from school sees you?"

Dylan snorted. "Hey, *I'm* the one with the new CD player." He turned and walked over to his bike. "You stay here and feel embarrassed if you want. I'm taking this stuff to the Quick Stop."

Well, Danielle thought, *money* is *money.* And it wasn't as though she had any better offers at the moment. "Wait up," she called after her brother. "I'll give you a hand."

Dylan handed her a pair of work gloves from his back pocket. "We'll fill up the crate on my bike. You ride it, and I'll carry the rest in the bag and ride yours."

A few minutes later, they were pedaling to the Quick Stop with their precious cargo. "Hold it!" Dylan hollered when they were halfway to the supermarket. Hopping off Danielle's bike, he hurried along the edge of the road, stopping to pick up four empty Coke cans. Then he ran back and hopped on the bike again, grinning.

So began Danielle's career in bottle hunting, or Conners Recycling Services, as her brother preferred to call it. Dylan found Danielle a crate like his and she rigged it onto her bike. It didn't take long for her to get the hang of the job. At first, scurrying around in ditches along the road and rooting through other people's garbage seemed a bit undignified. But once she got over that idea, it was sort of fun.

Dylan had a route mapped out that was already generating more returnables than he could carry himself. And then there were always new areas to explore.

Soon Danielle and her brother were competing with each other to see who could come home with more returnables. The two of them hadn't had this much fun together in a long time. It reminded Danielle of the Easter egg hunts she and Dylan had gone on when they were little kids.

More important, as Dylan had promised, the job really did pay off. For a couple hours' work every afternoon, Danielle could make ten or fifteen dollars, sometimes more. Only once did she fail to make less than ten dollars, and that was her first day. She learned the hard way that all cans and bottles are not created equal.

"Just stick with surefire things," Dylan advised. "Soda's the best." Cans were preferable to bottles, if you had a choice, since cans could be squashed down and took up less room than bottles. Stomping on cans was one of Danielle's favorite parts of the job.

Dylan had a real genius for spotting returnables among the roadside rocks and grassy rubble. Soon Danielle developed her own talent for spying cans and bottles. When the job got slow, she reminded herself that all of this was for a good cause, to make money so she could bring Redman home.

After two weeks of can collecting, plus two Friday nights baby-sitting the Stevens twins, a pair of towheaded brats belonging to some woman who worked with her mom, Danielle had added almost two hundred dollars to the Redman homecoming fund. She'd saved practically every penny except the money she spent on work gloves.

Some afternoons, the approach of darkness and the fear of being late for dinner were all that kept Danielle and Dylan from their collecting. They needed to make use of whatever time they could, because the weather wasn't exactly cooperating. Practically every day a thunderstorm seemed to blow up out of nowhere, drenching the central Florida highlands and then disappearing.

One afternoon, after such a storm, Danielle was

riding her bike along a little-used county road. Dylan had told her there were often good pickings to be found between the county road and the interstate. If a motorist on the highway threw something out his window it would roll down the embankment and come to rest in the ditch beside the county road, where it was easy to pick up.

Sure enough, there were at least a dozen cans in the ditch today, washed into a heap by the rain. It amazed Danielle how many pigs there were driving around Wishing Wells these days.

As she pedaled along, bottles and cans rattling and clanking in her basket, she came to the edge of a cow field. Not far from the road she saw an old oak tree that had been split nearly in half by a lightning bolt.

Danielle coasted to a stop, hopped off her bike, and walked over to the tree to check it out. The weight of the broken half had pulled part of the tree to the ground. It was still greenish-white inside. It must have been hit very recently.

She touched the sticky, splintered wood, running her fingers across the annual rings. Counting them, she figured the tree was about forty years old. Just as she was about to walk back to her bike, something half buried at her feet caught her eye.

The object was sticking up out of the wet dirt among some pieces of broken window glass.

Danielle bent down to touch it, then pulled it loose. It was a horseshoe. She held it up and wiped off some of the dirt.

It was the smallest horseshoe Danielle had ever seen, perhaps a shoe for a Shetland pony or maybe even some breed of miniature horse. It seemed to be made of bronze. When she rubbed off more dirt, a series of odd markings appeared along the flat side. They looked like words written in an unfamiliar alphabet or some strange code. Etched in the metal above the markings were three stars.

As Danielle stood in the field examining her find, a dreamlike sensation came over her. A gust of wind whispered through the hanging branches. "Merkain...Merkain..." it seemed to say.

Merkain...

The story Mr. Lyman had told her English class sprang into her mind—the Irish legend about the spirit horse and the fabled land of Valdor. There had been something else to the tale. Something about horseshoes. Magical horseshoes. *That's right!* Danielle realized excitedly. *Merkain's shoes were magic!*

Now she could remember Mr. Lyman saying: *Sometimes Merkain will throw a shoe during a thunderstorm and it will fall to Earth. People say that the lucky person who finds one of these magical horseshoes can invoke the Midnight Stallion and be granted three wishes.*

Danielle looked at the horseshoe again. Could it be? Right away, voices started arguing in her head.

Wouldn't it be great if there was something to that old story after all?

Right. And maybe there are fairies living in the tool shed.

But isn't it an awful lot of coincidences? Mr. Lyman's story, the lightning storm last night, and now this?

Danielle brushed more dirt off the horseshoe with the sleeve of her shirt.

Oh, come on, said one of the voices in her head. *Get rid of that stupid piece of junk and get back to work.*

Danielle gazed back at her bike and the pile of empty cans in the basket. She wasn't usually a dreamer, but sometimes...

Maybe it was just fun to imagine magic horses galloping around in the sky at night, Danielle told herself with a sigh.

A smile crept across her face. She sure could use a fairy-godmother horse granting her a few wishes. Just supposing...What would she ask for?

Lots of money, so her parents wouldn't have to work and she wouldn't have to go to school? *No,* she corrected herself. Even rich kids had to go to school.

Maybe she should make some "test wishes" first, just for fun. *Hmm,* Danielle thought. *Let's see...* How about wishing for something easy, like help with her homework? Or maybe something good to eat. Sure, why not?

Danielle held the horseshoe up to the sky. "Mighty steed Merkain, in the name of the Golden Horseshoe I command thee," she began, keeping her voice as low and official-sounding as she could make it. "By the heavens, grant me this wish—one clams linguini dinner with strawberries for dessert."

The wind whistled through the trees again, rattling the empty soda cans piled in Danielle's bike basket. She laughed at herself for being so superstitious and threw the tiny horseshoe into the basket with all the other junk she'd picked up by the road. Then she pedaled off, rattling, clinking, and clanking along as visions of the ghost horse Merkain danced in her head.

CHAPTER EIGHT

Horseshoe Head

Danielle could smell it all the way from the porch: Clams linguini. But she couldn't be sure until she could witness it herself. Sure enough, when she entered the kitchen, a saucepan full of clams linguini was bubbling away on the stove. She pinched her arm to make sure she wasn't dreaming and then just stood there, blinking. Her mom came in and saw her gawking at the stove.

Mrs. Conners gave Danielle a warm smile. "Your favorite tonight, hon. I know how hard you and Dylan are working with your little recycling business, and I thought you'd appreciate something special."

"B-but, Mom," Danielle stammered, "we only have pasta on Friday nights."

"Gee, Danielle," said Mrs. Conners, sounding a little surprised, "you seem as if you're upset about it. I thought clams linguini was your favorite meal."

"It is," Danielle managed to say. "I just wasn't expecting…"

"Well, there was a special on clams at the grocery store," her mom explained, adjusting the heat on the stove, "so I figured we could all use a little treat tonight." She gave the sauce a stir with a long-handled wooden spoon. "Smells good, doesn't it? That's the extra garlic I put in. Strawberries for dessert, too."

Danielle was stunned. *That's exactly what I wished for!* she thought. *It can't be!*

Mrs. Conners turned her attention back to the noodles. "Go on and wash up," she said over her shoulder. Danielle nodded weakly and climbed the stairs, barely feeling the steps beneath her feet.

Dylan met her halfway. "Hey, what's up, Danielle? You look kinda weird."

"I think I might be going crazy, that's all."

"So what else is new?" her brother quipped cheerfully.

Danielle pushed past him and headed to the bathroom. Splashing some water on her face, she gazed at her reflection in the bathroom mirror. *Did the horseshoe really make my wish come true? Was there such a thing as magic?*

By the time she came back downstairs, she was sure of just one thing: There was no way she was going to tell her mom or brother about the horseshoe. They wouldn't believe her anyway, and she didn't particularly feel like being laughed at. *Who could blame them?* Danielle thought. The whole thing sounded ridiculous. She could hardly believe it herself.

It must be some sort of coincidence, Danielle told herself. Had her mother mentioned something about clams and strawberries when Danielle had come home from school and she hadn't remembered? Or was there some other explanation?

All through dinner, Danielle stayed very quiet, answering only yes or no when her mom asked her questions about her day at school. In spite of being served her favorite meal, Danielle was so distracted she barely touched her food. She ended up sharing most of the clams with Dylan. Her mom gave her some concerned looks, but said nothing. After they finished doing the dishes, Mrs. Conners went to her office. Danielle and Dylan headed upstairs to their rooms.

Danielle dumped her schoolbooks on her desk and fished out the night's homework assignment. Focusing on math problems helped her to get her mind off things for a while. Plugging numbers into formulas and getting an answer that was either right or wrong seemed very comforting right now.

She'd left the horseshoe out in the tool shed, inside the basket with all the bottles and cans she'd brought back home when she ran out of time to take them to the Quick Stop. Something inside her wanted to take another look at it, to make sure it was really there and this whole thing wasn't all her wild imagination. But somehow she just couldn't bring herself to walk out to the tool shed. It was almost as if she was scared to go outside. After a while, though, she couldn't stand holding in the secret anymore.

Being careful that her mom and Dylan wouldn't overhear, she went downstairs to the kitchen and called Julie, telling her the whole story.

Julie, her supposed best friend, laughed, long and hard. "Give me a break, Danielle," she gasped between breaths. "You should hear yourself."

Danielle tightened her grip on the receiver. "Hey, I'm serious."

"That's why it's so funny." Julie laughed some more.

Danielle felt hurt, then angry. "Thanks for being so understanding, pal," she said hotly. "I'll talk to you later." She started to hang up the phone.

"Lighten up, Danielle," Julie managed between chuckles. "I'm sorry, okay?"

"Some best friend *you* are," Danielle grumbled.

"Hey, come on, it's just that you sound as if you really think some horseshoe had anything to do with what you had for dinner. Do you know how nuts that is? You don't really believe that some magical horse flies around in thunderstorms, do you? That was just a fairy tale Mr. Lyman told us."

"It was a legend," Danielle protested. "There's a difference."

"Well, lucky charms are stupid," Julie said. "They don't work."

"That sounds pretty strange coming from someone who wears a crystal around her neck," Danielle reminded her friend.

"Maybe so," Julie admitted, "but I know for a fact your mom makes clams linguini a lot. Didn't we have the same thing for dinner the last time I spent the night at your house?"

"Never on Tuesdays," Danielle insisted. "My mom always schedules our dinners. You know, like Meat Loaf Mondays and chicken on Wednesday? We get pasta on Fridays, and we haven't had clams linguini for at least a month."

Julie didn't answer right away. "You're really serious, aren't you?" she said finally. Some of the mocking tone had left her voice.

"I just think it's weird, that's all," Danielle said.

"Maybe. Still, I don't think you need to be scared or anything."

"I guess." Danielle sighed. "It must be a coincidence, like you say."

Julie giggled. "I'll tell you what, Danielle. Make another wish. Then you'll know for sure. Why don't you wish that I pass that math test Mr. Lee gave us today?"

"No way. Besides, that's too easy. You know you're going to pass, Julie."

Julie didn't sound so sure. "If you say so."

"No," Danielle said coolly. "I'm going to wish for Redman to come home."

"Mmm," Julie said. "Well, good luck, Danielle. I just don't want you to be disappointed, that's all."

"I won't be. See you, Julie."

They said good night, and Danielle went back upstairs to finish her homework. She went to bed at ten, feeling better after talking with her friend.

Another lightning storm arrived sometime after midnight. The sounds of thunder woke Danielle from her sleep. She lay in the dark, imagining a mysterious winged horse racing above the clouds. When she was snuggled up in her warm, cozy bed, the thought wasn't really so scary. Her great-great-grandparents had been Irish, after all. If there really was anything to those old stories, what would Merkain have against a nice Irish-American girl like her?

After the storm passed, Danielle was awakened again by a noise outside her bedroom. There was a light on in the hall. Her brother was moaning and groaning and running back and forth between his room and the bathroom. After the second or third time, Danielle heard her mom get up and start rustling around in the medicine cabinet. Then Mrs. Conners told Dylan to take some medicine for his stomach. "I'm so sorry, honey," she said.

Danielle couldn't help but feel sorry for her

brother. He could be a real pain when he wanted to, but the truth was that the two of them were very close.

She stared up at the ceiling. If her wish yesterday really *did* have anything to do with having linguini for dinner, was it her fault that the clams had made Dylan sick? She rolled over and closed her eyes, telling herself to forget about everything until tomorrow.

In the morning, Dylan looked a little green. "I never want to see another clam as long as I live," he grumbled, getting his books together for school.

After breakfast Danielle went out to the tool shed and found the mysterious horseshoe among the bottles she'd collected. The whole wish thing seemed pretty dumb in the cold light of a school-day morning.

It's just an old horseshoe, she told herself. *Nothing more.* But what were those markings etched in the metal? she wondered. They looked like some kind of secret code. And those stars...Suddenly, she gasped, nearly dropping the horseshoe. *One of the stars had turned green overnight!*

A shiver ran up Danielle's spine. What if she wished for Redman to come home and her horse ended up getting sick like Dylan? How could she risk causing something like that to happen? The safest thing to do would be to make another test wish before asking Merkain about Redman. That way, she'd still have one wish left. And by then, maybe she'd have a better idea of what she was dealing with.

What should I wish for? Danielle asked herself.

A new CD player like Dylan's? Help doing her research paper? Or how about wishing for Mr. Lyman to come back? All the possibilities made her head spin.

Julie was already at the bus stop when Danielle arrived. She quickly told her friend what had happened.

Julie waggled her fingers. "Ooh," she kidded her friend. "Next thing you're gonna tell me, you were abducted by space aliens."

"All right, Ms. Crystal Power..."

"Horseshoe Head," Julie teased back.

"Okay, okay," Danielle said. "Truce. But I'm telling you," she insisted, "one of those stars turned green overnight."

"It was probably green all along and you didn't notice," Julie said.

Danielle was pretty sure all the stars had been gold when she first rubbed the dirt off the horseshoe. But thinking back, she couldn't be absolutely positive. Maybe Julie was right.

Julie changed the subject. "So, are you and Dylan going bottle hunting this afternoon?"

"I don't know about Dylan. He still looked pretty

sick this morning. But, yeah, I'm going. It's not like I have a whole lot of other options." Danielle glanced down the road toward the oncoming school bus. "Maybe that'll change soon, though."

Julie raised her eyebrows. "Oh really?"

"Don't laugh," Danielle said, "I made another wish."

Julie shook her head in disbelief. "I really don't think you should mess around with this stuff," she said, sounding worried. "What if there really *is* something to that horseshoe? It could be dangerous."

"It's not any different from making a wish on a birthday cake or a falling star," Danielle pointed out. "Nobody gets too worked up about that."

"I guess, if you put it that way," Julie said slowly.

The school bus lumbered to a stop, and Julie and Danielle lined up with the other kids waiting to climb aboard.

"Okay, then," said Julie, as they took their regular seat at the back. "So when is Redman coming home?"

"I didn't wish for Redman to come home. I decided to try another test wish first."

Julie giggled. "This is great. What did you wish for this time? Money?"

Danielle took a deep breath. "I wished for Prima and Little Buddy to come back to the farm. I want my old job again."

Another Try

There was no sign of Prima or Little Buddy over the next few days. Danielle was beginning to feel discouraged. Had her first "test wish" been a coincidence after all? It sure looked that way.

The recycling business had turned slow, too. Or maybe it was just that some of the zeal Danielle had felt at first was wearing off. It was getting harder and harder to find enough bottles to fill up her basket. She and Dylan were covering much of the same territory. Her brother never complained, but Danielle knew she was cutting into his profits.

The farm was still quiet, although Danielle was getting used to it by now. Alec came and went. He was usually up and gone from the farm well before sunrise, and he often didn't return until long after dark.

She managed a library visit in town to check out the Florida history section for her English report.

While she was there, she picked up a book of Irish myths from the reserve shelf. It was an oversized, dusty old volume that looked as if it hadn't been touched in years. She opened the book and started to read. By the time she looked up again, the library was closing and she hadn't even looked at one book on Florida history.

That Friday, her baby-sitting job fell through at the last minute. Julie spent the night, and the two of them stayed up late watching TV. Danielle told Julie about the book of myths she found at the library. "There were some terrific illustrations inside," Danielle said.

"Sounds cool," Julie said. "Did it say anything about your friend Merkain?"

"No," Danielle said. "I did read about the Kelpies, though. Have you ever heard of them?"

Julie shook her head. "Nope."

"Well, Kelpies are ghost horses that take anyone who tries to ride them for a wild gallop to their deaths at the bottom of the sea."

"How cheery," Julie said, reaching into a bowl of popcorn.

"You know, I was thinking that sounds a lot like the way Mr. Lyman described Merkain. I bet Merkain was some sort of Kelpie."

"Sure, Danielle," Julie smirked. "Give it up, girl."

After breakfast the next morning, the two of

them walked out to the tool shed and were immediately attacked by Dylan's pet ferrets. Tiki leapt up at Julie and swung from her pants leg. The other one, Lulu, hissed and gave Danielle a playful nip on the ankle.

"Hey!" Danielle said, jumping back.

"Dylan!" Julie called. "Help!"

Dylan came running. "Get down, you two," he chided his polecats.

Danielle and Julie played with the furry troublemakers, watching them roughhouse and chase each other around the tool shed. Suddenly, Danielle heard the low groan of a heavy truck shifting gears. The sound came closer. They all went outside and saw the South Wind horse van rumbling up the driveway, then backing up to the paddock. Alec was behind the wheel.

Dylan glanced at Danielle and raised his eyebrows. It was unusual for Alec to show up here at this time of day, much less driving the South Wind van. "What's going on?" Dylan asked.

Danielle shrugged, just as confused as her brother.

Alec jumped quickly out of the van and swung open the paddock gate.

Danielle waved. "Hey, Alec," she called.

"Hey," Alec called back, nodding to Julie and Dylan.

Danielle followed Alec around the side of the van. He started settling the ramp into place, fitting the wings on each side of the ramp.

"What's up, Alec?" Danielle asked. She peered inside the van and could barely believe her eyes. "Is that Prima and Little Buddy in there?"

Alec winked. "Maybe so."

"But I thought you said they weren't coming back."

Alec's expression hardened. "Danielle, a couple of horses in one of the barns over at South Wind have come down with the flu. The vet wants to quarantine the place, but it's still too early to say whether any of the other horses are infected. Our horses weren't exposed, and I plan on keeping it that way."

"Is the flu serious?" Danielle asked.

Alec gave a wary nod. "Could be. To be safe I'm moving all our horses out of there until the situation gets sorted out. We can stable Prima and Little Buddy here, just like before. I've found stalls at a friend's barn in Ocala that will serve as temporary quarters for the Black and the two-year-olds in training."

Danielle was in shock. Prima and Little Buddy were back! *Wish number two had come true!*

"So I can have my old job back?" Danielle asked cautiously.

"Of course, Danielle," said Alec. "If you want it."

Danielle had to keep herself from jumping up

and down like a little kid. "This is great!"

Alec gave Danielle a sidelong glance. "Well, I don't know if I'd say *that*."

Danielle suddenly realized how selfish she was sounding. "I'm sorry, Alec. I didn't mean...I meant... I feel really bad some of the horses are sick."

Alec held up his hands. "I know you do, Danielle. Hey, there's no need to panic yet. It could be just a few isolated cases. Then again, it might be a full-fledged epidemic, affecting the whole state. The vet thinks everything is under control, but Henry's not taking any chances. For the immediate future, all that means is that we'll have our stock spread out over half the county." Alec sighed. "I'll be running from one farm to the next like a chicken with my head cut off until this flu bug runs its course."

"How long will that take?" Danielle asked.

Alec shrugged. "Could be days, weeks, even a month. We'll just have to wait and see."

One of the horses in the van began to whinny. "Let's get them unloaded," Alec said, swinging open the van doors and stepping inside.

Danielle glanced at Julie. One wish coming true could easily have been a coincidence. But *two*? For once, Julie didn't have some smart, know-it-all explanation.

With a flurry of hoofbeats, Prima and Little Buddy skittered down the ramp. "Hey, you guys!"

Danielle called to the horses. "Did you miss me, Little Buddy? How're you doing?" The colt took a little hop and then pawed the ground, his ears nervous and twitchy, his eyes bright. "That's my guy," Danielle said, smiling.

With the familiar smells and sounds of the horses, the farm seemed to come to life again. Alec turned the horses out into the lower pasture. Danielle and Julie hung over the fence to watch Prima and the colt prancing around. The horses didn't seem to have any worries. They were happy as long as there was grass to eat and room to run. *Who cares? Who cares?* sang their galloping feet.

"They look healthy enough," Danielle said.

"I hope so," Julie said. "I can't believe they're back. You are *so* lucky, Danielle."

Danielle sighed. "If only Redman were here, too. Then everything would be perfect."

"I bet you'll have your hands full with Prima and Buddy as it is," Julie said.

"Mmmm." Danielle was thinking about something else. "You know what? I'm two for two, Julie. I have one wish left on Merkain's lucky horseshoe. Redman's definitely coming home."

"Yeah, maybe," Julie said. "But think of the consequences, Danielle. Whenever you wish on that horseshoe, something bad happens, too. First you got your favorite dinner, but Dylan got sick. Then you got Prima and Little Buddy back, but the flu virus started. If that's magic, it's the wrong kind. This whole horseshoe thing gives me the creeps."

Danielle thought hard about that. What her friend said was true. More than anything in the world, she wanted her Redman home again. But she did feel guilty for profiting from the flu epidemic at South Wind. She couldn't help feeling responsible somehow.

Again she noticed how healthy Prima and Little Buddy looked. *Why do some horses get sick and others don't?* she wondered. Probably a lot of reasons, just as with people. Out in the pasture, Little Buddy began neighing loudly and charging around his mother. Danielle smiled. *Quit worrying so much,* she told herself. *Everything's fine.* The horses were back, and she had a job again.

"Hey, Danielle," Alec called. "Give me a hand unpacking Prima's tack trunk, will you?"

"Well, I've got to go," Julie said. "My mom will be looking for me." Danielle gave her friend a hug and waved as Julie rode off on her bike.

The colt was zigzagging about the pasture, whirling this way and that. Danielle watched him for a moment, feeling happier than she had in a long while. Then she went into the barn to help Alec and Billy unpack the trunks.

Changes

The next few days passed quickly for Danielle. She called Mrs. Stevens to give up her baby-sitting job and turned her half of the recycling business over to Dylan. She wanted to spend every minute of her free time with the horses.

Now Danielle had finished Little Buddy's lesson with the lead line. She and the colt were chasing each other around the pasture. Even though they were having fun, nagging thoughts ran through Danielle's mind. Last Thursday, Alec had brought some bad news from South Wind. "The flu outbreak is taking a turn for the worse," he had said. "Five more horses turned up sick. And at least one of the cases may be life-threatening."

It's not my fault, Danielle told herself. *Or is it?*

Over and over she kept thinking the same thing: *How can some old Irish legend have anything to do with me?* She had only one wish left. Did she dare wish for Redman? Would anyone else be hurt? Should she take the chance?

Danielle caught her breath and smiled at Little Buddy as he danced about the pasture. She called to him and set out across the pasture again at a trot. Behind her, she heard the rhythmic beat of hoofs. The colt rushed by her and slid to a stop. He turned to face her momentarily, then took off again. Danielle ran in another direction. With a snort, the colt turned around and ran after her.

They raced from one end of the pasture to the other. Finally, Danielle stopped and bent over, panting. The colt stopped beside her. "You win," Danielle told him. When she straightened up again, he shoved his nose into her hand.

"Sorry, Little Buddy," Danielle said. "No treats until we get back to the barn." The colt badgered her a while longer, then wandered off toward the corner of the pasture, where his mama was enjoying the warm sunshine. Soon he had joined Prima cropping grass.

For well over a month now, the colt had been eating grass, grazing with his long legs spread far apart and slightly bent so that he could reach the ground. It was only since he'd returned from South Wind that he was really developing a taste for it and not just trying to imitate his mother.

The colt galloped about the pasture again. Every

day he seemed to be running a little faster, jumping a little higher. His play was becoming rougher, too. The colt was a high-spirited young animal. Danielle wondered if one day someone would try to break that spirit. She hoped not. Alec certainly didn't seem like the type to do that. But he wouldn't allow the big colt to push him around, either. The Black himself was barely tame, yet Alec seemed to get what he wanted from the stallion without being rough.

Little Buddy whirled suddenly and sped off to the other end of the pasture. Danielle watched him settle into a gallop, his gait long and low and sweeping. The colt slid to a stop, spun around and ran back toward Danielle. Five yards away, he swerved like a football player running for a touchdown. He celebrated reaching the end of the pasture by flinging his hind legs in the air with reckless abandon.

"You nutball," Danielle called, shaking her head. It was funny, she thought. Somehow it seemed that she'd known the colt forever, but it had been barely two months. School had just been starting when Little Buddy first arrived at the farm. He'd been four months old then, his legs long and spindly. They were still long, but they weren't so skinny now. Every passing week, the fine lines of his young muscles were filling out. His delicate head held large eyes that were fired with excitement, and the white star on his forehead was becoming more defined.

Nearly six months old now, the colt was no longer a baby. He weighed more than five hundred pounds, stood over thirteen hands, and ate eight to ten quarts of feed daily and still looked for more. With all the oats and hay he ate to keep him going, Little Buddy no longer needed his mother's milk. Like every other foal born this year, he would be considered a yearling on January first, and that wasn't far away. Soon he'd have to start acting like one. There would be no more running to Prima for protection when he felt scared or lonely.

Alec was waiting for Danielle by the paddock when she brought Prima and the colt in from the pasture. "Everything okay?" he asked.

Danielle wasn't sure if Alec was asking about her or the colt. She nodded. "Yeah, we're fine. He just about wore me out, though."

Alec gave the colt a pat on the neck. "Who's my guy? Are you giving your girlfriend a hard time, Little Buddy?"

Little Buddy tossed his head in answer.

They led Prima and Little Buddy over to the walking path and slowly circled the barn. The mare nickered softly. Danielle smiled, reaching out to touch her fine, soft muzzle. "That's my girl," Danielle said. Prima pulled away. With a snort, she swung her head to gaze longingly off in the direction of the upper pasture.

"Prima really likes it here," Alec said. "She's going to miss it."

Danielle felt a chill run up her spine. Did Alec mean what she thought he did? *Not again,* she thought. "Are the horses going somewhere?" she asked slowly.

"Just Prima," Alec said. "Tomorrow's the colt's big day. Mama's leaving."

Danielle looked over at the mare, who had turned her head into the wind. Did Prima sense the changes to come? she wondered.

"It's the right time, I think," Alec said softly.

Danielle bit her lip. She should have expected this. Little Buddy had reached the time in his life when he had to leave his mother. It was the natural order of things, Danielle knew. Somehow, she had pushed that hard fact to the back of her mind. But at least she wasn't losing the colt again, too. "Where are you taking her?" Danielle asked. "She can't go back to South Wind yet, can she?"

"I found a farm a couple of miles away where I can board her until South Wind is safe again." Concern entered Alec's voice. "I'm afraid things aren't improving much over there. Charlie Moyer's filly might not make it through the night. And two other horses are nearly as bad off."

Danielle felt a pang of heartache for the sick horses. What could she do to help? She forced herself to turn her attention back to Alec and the colt.

"Is there anything I can do for Little Buddy tomorrow?" Danielle asked. "He's such a mama's boy. I'd really like to be there with him."

"Don't you have school?" Alec asked.

Danielle shrugged. "My class is taking a field trip to Busch Gardens in Tampa tomorrow. If I explain the situation, I think Mom will write me an excuse so I can stay home. Busch Gardens is no big deal to me. Besides, Dad took Julie and me there last summer. I've been on all the rides already."

"Okay, then," Alec said. "I could certainly use the extra help. I'm sure the colt will appreciate a friendly face, too."

Danielle smiled. "It's a deal."

Alec held up a hand. "Whoa, slow down, Danielle. First you'd better check with your mom. In the meantime, you can help me get these horses bedded down for the night. They're in for a busy day tomorrow."

The next morning, the horses were fed, given a light grooming, and then turned out to pasture. Danielle cleaned up around the barn. In between chores, she watched Prima and the colt grazing in the pasture, seemingly uninterested in anything beyond the pasture fence.

Alec walked into the barn, and Danielle followed him into the tack room.

"Have you heard any news from South Wind?"

Alec shrugged. "Moyer's filly made it through the night." He glanced toward the pasture. "But it's our guy out there we have to be concerned with right now. Let's get Prima's trunk packed up, okay? Billy will be here soon with the van."

Danielle gave a nod and did as she was told.

"It's going to be plenty noisy around here for a day or so," Alec warned. "I hope you and your family are ready for it."

They set to work. Danielle folded Prima's new cooler, then started gathering up all of the mare's personal gear, from buckets to bridles.

When they were finished, Danielle walked outside. The colt was racing to the far end of the pasture, completely ignoring his mother's pleas for him to return. Maybe separating the two of them now wouldn't be so hard on the colt after all.

Soon Danielle heard the horse van rumbling up the driveway. She saw Billy's lean face, dark mustache, and cowboy hat through the windshield.

Carrying a bucket of feed, Alec enticed the horses from the pasture to the barn. Little Buddy was moved to the new stall Alec had prepared for him while Prima was clipped to the cross-ties in the corridor. The colt eyed his new surroundings suspiciously. Then he gave a snort and whinnied a few times, showing his indignation at having his playtime interrupted.

"Why is Buddy getting the new stall, Alec?" Danielle asked. "Will the old one remind him of Prima?"

"Yeah," Alec said, "that's one reason. I think the new stall's a little safer, too."

"Safer?" Danielle repeated, confused.

At first glance, Little Buddy's new stall looked exactly like his old one. It was directly across the corridor from the stall he had shared with Prima and identical to it in every way, except that all the feed pails and water buckets had been removed.

"It's going to get real crazy in here when Little Buddy realizes what's going on," Alec explained. "Anything the colt might crash into when he starts popping off has to go."

The colt whinnied a few more times, then stopped. It wasn't the first time he had been isolated from his mother. The two of them had been apart for short periods around the barn, to be groomed and bathed, and during the colt's lessons. Danielle watched Little Buddy as he sniffed at the straw bedding spread on the floor. He had no way of knowing that this wasn't going to be just a temporary separation, like all the others.

This one would last the rest of his life.

The Weanling

While Danielle held Prima's lead, Alec buckled the plaid stable sheet into place and set to work wrapping the mare's legs in shipping bandages. "You want them snug but not too tight," Alec said as Danielle watched.

Prima looked searchingly around. The mare probably suspected something was up because of this change in her daily routine, Danielle thought. Billy set to work getting the van ready. As usual, the tall, thin man worked in silence, almost seeming to melt into the background. His eyes were hidden by the dark aviator sunglasses that seemed to be permanently glued to his face.

"Okay, Danielle," Alec said finally. "Your job is to stay here with Little Buddy. He shouldn't be able to hurt himself inside that stall, but keep an eye on him just in case."

Danielle nodded. "Got it."

Alec took the mare's lead, clucked softly to her and led her out the barn door. Danielle was left alone with the colt, who by now was beginning to guess what was happening. His short, shrill neighs came frequently as he moved back and forth in the large stall. His ears were pricked, his eyes large and startled.

Danielle opened the stall door and went inside to comfort him. She called to him, but he ignored her outstretched hand and the carrot pieces she offered. "That's okay, fella. I understand," Danielle said sympathetically. It was true. She knew all too well what it was like to be separated suddenly from someone you loved.

Outside the barn, she heard a few sad neighs from Prima, then the sound of hoofs on the ramp leading into the van. The doors banged closed, and the mare neighed again as the van motor started. Her muffled cries grew fainter as the van began pulling out of the driveway.

Frantically, Little Buddy paced about the stall. His cries sounded desperate. Danielle stood beside the half doors of the stall, wanting to comfort him but knowing she couldn't take his mama's place.

Suddenly, the colt rushed the door. Rearing on his hind legs, he threw up his forelegs in an attempt to get over the half door.

Instinctively, Danielle reached beneath his hard

body in time to stop him. Somehow she found the strength to hold him back and pull his struggling legs from the door.

When the colt's hoofs were on the ground again, Danielle hurriedly closed the wire-mesh screen above the half door. *This is dangerous,* she told herself. There was no way she could stay in the stall if he kept acting up like this. Once again Little Buddy resumed his neighing, pacing back and forth. His eyes never left the barn door as he watched impatiently for the mare to return.

"It's all right, Little Buddy. It's all right," Danielle whispered. But the terror in the colt's eyes told her that nothing she could say mattered to him at the moment. His whole world had just been shattered.

When Alec returned an hour later, Danielle was still inside the stall. The colt's incessant neighing rang throughout the barn, as plaintive and lost a cry as Danielle had ever heard. Alec stood for a moment, watching the colt. Then he went to the grain box and returned with a quart of oats.

"Put this in his box," Alec said to Danielle. "Maybe we can distract him a bit." But the colt showed no interest in the grain. His eyes never left the closed barn door as he stood vigil, waiting for his mother.

"You might as well come out now, Danielle,"

Alec said finally. "This will go on all day, and nothing we can do is going to help."

Danielle shook her head firmly. "I want to stay," she said. "If you think it's all right," she added quickly.

Alec shrugged. "It's up to you. You know enough about horses to keep from getting hurt. Seeing him suffer will be tough to watch, though."

Danielle told Alec about the colt rushing the door as the van was leaving. Alec checked the colt's legs for bruises or other injuries.

"I should have figured he'd try something like that," Alec said. He sounded a little angry with himself. "I probably should have wrapped his legs, too. We're lucky he didn't get hurt. You either, for that matter."

"We're both okay, aren't we, Little Buddy?" Danielle said. The colt flicked an ear at the mention of his name but otherwise maintained his vigil.

"Is it always like this with weanlings?" Danielle asked.

Alec nodded. "Some are worse than others. I have a feeling this colt will be putting up more of a fuss than most. He's hardly as timid as most of the others his age. There's a lot of the Black in him. That could make him hard to handle if we're not careful. I only hope he'll learn to save his energy for the racetrack and not use it up fighting us."

Danielle wished she could do something to ease the pain of separation the colt was enduring. It seemed so unfair. Then she thought about the mare.

"What about Prima?" Danielle asked. "How long will she miss Little Buddy? Days? Weeks? Months? Forever?"

Alec shook his head. "Not long, once she's been reunited with the other mares. In a couple days, she'll forget all about her foal, the same way Little Buddy will forget about his mother."

Danielle's eyes. "Really?"

"Sure. That's the way it should be. His life will soon be very busy and full all on its own. We have big plans for this guy."

Little Buddy's unanswered cries echoed through the barn. Danielle leaned against the stall door and tried to imagine him at a racetrack. Right now it was hard to see anything but a scared little colt pining for his mama. His future life as a champion racehorse seemed very far off.

Danielle stayed with Little Buddy the entire day, except for a few minutes in the late afternoon when she went inside the house to grab a sandwich. She tried to soothe him as best as she could, telling him about Redman and all the fun the three of them were going to have together when the big paint returned home. Alec checked in on the colt every couple of hours or so.

Once in a while, Danielle gave the colt some sugar or a piece of carrot. When he had eaten the treat, she took him by his halter and tried to lead him to the corner feed box and the rack of hay. He always refused, turning his head to the door and thrashing his tail. His eyes were still frightened. Danielle kept running her hands over his coat and talking softly to him.

Just before dinner, Alec showed up to relieve her, and Danielle slipped out of the stall. For the first time since Prima's disappearance, Little Buddy had stopped his wailing for more than a few minutes. He pressed his muzzle hard against the screen, the better to see what was going on outside.

"He'll quiet down soon enough," Alec said.

"What about tonight?" Danielle asked.

"Oh, he'll start up again. But I'll be with him. And he'll be exhausted from all the moving around. He'll sleep. They all do."

"You're *sleeping* here?" Danielle asked.

Alec nodded. "Yeah. there isn't really any need for it. It's just something I like to do on their first night alone."

"Could I stay here too?" Danielle asked.

Alec shook his head. "I don't know how your mom would feel about that. Don't worry so much, Danielle. Everything will be fine." He turned his attention back to the colt. "That's my guy," Alec cooed gently. "Did you hear that? Everything's going to be all right, Little Buddy."

There was almost a bold, arrogant look about the colt as he peered outside. Danielle smiled. "He looks okay now."

"Well, don't be fooled," Alec told her. "There's a long, hard night ahead. He'll remember standing close to his mama, safe and protected by her big body. He won't feel so tough then."

When Alec left to make a telephone call, Danielle stayed to watch Little Buddy until the clang of the dinner bell told her it was time for her to go in. The colt bobbed his head and thrashed his tail as she closed the stall door behind her. "Don't be mad, Little Buddy," she said. "I'll be back later."

Stepping outside into the cool, clear night, Danielle hurried across the driveway and through the yard to the house. Her mom and Dylan were already in the kitchen, getting ready to eat. Danielle ran upstairs to wash her hands and then joined them at the kitchen table. Mrs. Conners listened to Danielle's report on Prima's departure and the condition of the colt.

"For a while there, it sounded like someone was being murdered in the barn," her brother said, between bites of bread.

Danielle stirred her soup. "Well, it's not over yet."

"Poor little thing," said Mrs. Conners sympathetically. "He's going to have a rough night."

"I thought I might sit up with him awhile, if that's okay, Mom."

"After your homework's finished," Mrs. Conners said. "And don't stay up too late. Remember, tomorrow's a school day."

Danielle helped with the dishes, then ran up to her room to hit the books. Her English report was finally starting to take shape. She opened another research book and started to read about the war with the Seminole Indians, trying to ignore the sad cries coming from the barn. Poor Little Buddy was neighing himself hoarse. Danielle had to grin in spite of herself. A hoarse horse.

She glanced out the window and saw that Alec had turned on all the barn lights. But the brightness wasn't fooling Little Buddy. A terribly frightening darkness surrounded him, and he didn't want any part of it. His heartbreaking calls for his mother filled the night. Occasionally there would be a lull in his cries, but then the desperate whinnies would start all over again. It was just about the saddest sound Danielle had ever heard.

She finished her homework and hurried down to the barn. Alec wasn't there. She figured he was working in the Coop, or maybe catching a nap before the long night ahead. Buddy welcomed her by lashing his tail and pawing the ground. Then he went back to his braying. "So it's going to be like this, is it?" Danielle chided him.

She'd brought her research book to read while she baby-sat Buddy. In it was a picture of a Seminole Indian riding a horse that looked a lot like Redman. At least Danielle thought so. She showed Buddy the picture to get his opinion, then read aloud to him a section about a chief named Osceola who fought the United States Army and never surrendered.

As the minutes passed, Danielle realized that the drone of her voice was helping quiet the colt. When she finished, the colt sniffed the book, then snorted in disgust. Danielle pulled the book away and stepped out of the stall into the aisle. "Come on, Buddy," she said. "It's not *that* bad."

Propping herself up on a tack trunk just outside the stall door, she continued to read aloud. Buddy remained on his feet, pacing about his stall. He wanted no part of the comfortable straw bedding. He had no time for sleep. He wanted his mama.

"Easy, Little Buddy," Danielle repeated drowsily for the hundredth time, but the colt's eyes remained wide open.

Near midnight, Alec arrived, carrying a fold-up cot under one arm. "Go and get some sleep, Danielle," he said. "I'll take over here."

Danielle quickly put down her book. "No way,"

she said. "I mean...um, couldn't I stay a little longer?"

Alec smiled. "You don't want to be falling asleep in class tomorrow, do you?" Buddy started whinnying again, louder than ever, as if to second the motion for Danielle to leave. She looked at the colt and sighed. She had told herself that she wouldn't go to sleep until the colt did, but from the way he was behaving, that could be quite a while.

"All right, all right," she said. "I can take the hint, you guys. I'm out of here." Stifling a yawn, she gave the colt one final pat on the neck. "Good night, Little Buddy."

Alec gave her a nod. "Good work, Danielle. Go get some sleep, now."

"Good night, Alec," she said, and walked over to the house. Once she was in bed, she fell asleep almost before her head hit the pillow.

Sometime near morning, Danielle woke and sat up in bed. Outside her window, the faintest blue was beginning to color the black sky. Something had just happened, she knew. But what? Then she heard it. Or *didn't* hear it, more exactly.

Quiet had finally descended on the barn.

CHAPTER TWELVE

Waiting

Getting out of bed, Danielle stumbled sleepily down the hall to the bathroom. A minute later she had dressed and made her bed and was creeping quietly downstairs to eat a quick bowl of cereal.

The farm was bathed in gray, misty light as she ran out to the barn. Alec was still there, asleep, slouched over on top of the tack trunk. The fold-up cot was leaning against the grain box, untouched. *The poor guy must have been up all night,* Danielle thought.

The colt eyed Danielle and gave a brief whinny. Alec grunted and jerked his head slightly. Danielle looked at the colt and put a finger to her lips. "Shh," she told him. "Alec's trying to sleep."

She wondered if she should give the colt his breakfast. *Better not,* she thought. There was no telling what Alec had planned for him today. The colt still looked scared, though his eyes were showing less of the terror that had filled them the night before.

Danielle heard another stirring sound behind her and turned around. Alec sat up and set his feet on the ground. His clothes were rumpled, his hair in his face. He wiped a hand across his eyes and got up without noticing Danielle, then walked outside to stretch and splash water on his hands and face.

Danielle picked up a broom and was about to start sweeping up the tack room when Alec walked back in and finally saw her. He shook his head, bewildered. "What are you doing here, Danielle? Your mom thinks you spend too much time hanging around the barn as it is. Get to school, will you?"

Danielle bent down to sweep a pile of dirt into a dustpan. "I just wanted to see Little Buddy for a second," she said.

"He's fine, Danielle. You don't have to worry about a thing, believe me." Outside, a car had pulled up the driveway. *Billy,* Danielle thought. A door slammed, and the lanky cowboy strode into the barn, his morning chaw of tobacco bulging in one cheek and his sunglasses already firmly in place.

Danielle waved. Billy acknowledged her with a nod, then walked over to Alec, who was leaning against Little Buddy's stable door.

"Rough night?" Danielle heard him ask Alec.

Alec shrugged. "Not bad. He's still sweating it

some, but the worst should be over soon."

"Are you going to turn them out today?" Danielle asked.

Billy looked over his shoulder. "You still here, kid?"

"I'm going, Billy, don't worry. I have plenty of time to make the bus."

Billy scowled at her from behind his bug-eyed shades. Alec shook his head sleepily and shrugged. Sometimes Danielle wondered if Billy objected to having a kid hanging around the barn all the time. He certainly wouldn't cut her any slack, the way Alec might, and for days after the lightning episode, he'd hounded her about not fixing the fence. But as long as Danielle did her chores and stayed out of the way, Billy usually treated her okay.

"I was just wondering how you were going to handle Little Buddy today, that's all."

"Easy," Billy said, taking his glasses off and studying them a moment. "Nice and easy."

Alec scratched the back of his neck. "We'll probably keep him in the barn today. Maybe tomorrow, too. The colt is still really keyed up," he explained. "We don't want him to hurt himself."

Billy nodded. "Wouldn't surprise me if he threw another tantrum or two before the day is over."

"Hopefully he'll be pretty well settled down by the time you get back from school, Danielle," Alec said. "You'll see him then. Now get out of here, would you?"

Danielle brought her hand to her forehead in a playful salute. "Yes, sir!" She went over to say good-bye to Little Buddy, pressing her face up to the screened top half of the stall door. There was a half-sick, half-crazy look in the colt's eyes. The terror of his first night alone without his mother was obviously very fresh in his mind.

"Everything's gonna be all right, Little Buddy," she reassured him. "You'll see." The colt looked far from convinced, his eyes fixed and staring, his muscles quivering. Then she turned and ran from the barn to get her bike before Alec or Billy could start barking at her again.

CHAPTER THIRTEEN

Vanished!

The farm was quiet when Danielle arrived home. There was barely a whinny from the direction of the barn. She took a liter bottle of soda from the refrigerator and poured herself a glass, emptying it in a few gulps. There was a bag of raw vegetables on the bottom shelf. She picked out a couple of carrots, broke them in half, and stuck them in her jacket pocket.

"Dylan? Is that you?" her mom called from upstairs.

"It's me, Mom," said Danielle, rinsing her glass and dropping it in the drainer next to the sink.

"Come here a second, will you?" Mrs. Conners asked.

Danielle clomped up the stairs and looked in the office door. Her mom was hunched over her desk, examining a drawing. Mrs. Conners looked up from her sketch and beckoned. "How was school?"

"Okay. What's up?"

"Oh, nothing special. I just wanted to see you." Mrs. Conners spun around in her chair and stood to give her daughter a hug. "How's your little colt making out?"

Danielle looked anxiously out the window. "You tell me, Mom. I've been in school all day."

"It's been pretty quiet, for the most part."

"Really?" Danielle asked. "I wonder if that's a good sign or a bad one."

Mrs. Conners frowned. "Wait. I take that back. He did start up around noon for a half hour or so. Billy's been here most of the day, I think. Alec's truck has come and gone a few times, too."

"I guess I'll find out what's up soon enough."

Mrs. Conners pushed back a few strands of blond hair from Danielle's face and smiled. Danielle peeked over her mother's shoulder at the drawing. It was a circular wheel design, with two interlocking gears.

"It's nothing much right now, part of a cover sketch for a CD." Danielle's mom gave a little sigh. "I can't really seem to get going on it."

"Who's it for?"

"Some friends of your father's. They have a band called Big Wheelie and the Motorheads. Ever hear of them?"

Danielle shook her head as her mother adjusted

the movable lamp over her desk. "Me neither," she said. "They need a new logo, something mechanical-looking. I don't even know what a flywheel looks like. I thought maybe Dylan could help."

Danielle nodded. "Yeah, he's good with that sort of thing."

Mrs. Conners pulled a fresh piece of paper from her notepad. Danielle said good-bye and headed straight for the barn. Billy was there, wrestling bales of hay from the back of his pickup.

"Here comes trouble," he said in his cowboy drawl.

"Sounds might-ee quiet around here," Danielle replied, doing her best impersonation of Billy's accent. Just as the words were out of her mouth, the barn erupted with a series of shrill whinnies. The colt was crying for his mother. *And also because he's sick of being penned up all day,* Danielle thought. Then she smiled to herself. *He probably likes to hear his own voice, too.*

Billy tossed the last bale from the truck and went into the barn.

"So, are you going to turn Buddy loose tomorrow?" Danielle asked eagerly, following him.

Billy took off his aviator shades. "Maybe. We'll see how he does tonight."

Little Buddy gave another cry. "It's sort of sad to see him all penned up," Danielle said. Billy shrugged.

"Do you really think it's safe in here for him?" Danielle asked.

"It won't hurt that little troublemaker to stay inside another day or so," Billy said.

Danielle was surprised. The colt was so young and strong. To her, it seemed that it would be more dangerous to keep him cooped up in the barn.

"But don't you think..."

"This is the way it's done, Danielle," Billy said, sounding as if he was starting to lose patience. "When he leaves here, the only thing we want him to have on his mind is going out to play. We don't want him running off on some half-cocked search for his mom."

"Oh," Danielle said, still doubtful.

"In a month or so, the colt would be able to walk right by Prima without so much as a whinny. But right now..."

"You don't really think he could jump the pasture fence to try and track down Prima, do you?"

"No," Billy said. "But he could sure hurt himself trying."

Danielle peeked into Little Buddy's stall. "Hey, Big Guy. You feelin' better now? I told you everything would be okay, didn't I?"

The colt pressed his nose up against the partition.

"Just look at all the company you've been getting," Danielle told him. "There's Billy over there. And Alec. And me."

The colt stared at Danielle. Then he took a turn around his stall and stopped to gaze longingly out the window at the shady trees around his favorite playing areas in the upper pasture.

"Don't worry, Little Buddy. It won't be long now." Danielle turned to Billy. "Anything I can do to help?"

"Sure. Take a walk out there in the pasture and pick up any dead branches that might have blown down from the trees. Look for anything that the colt might fall on or start messing with when we finally do turn him out."

Danielle nodded and set off to the pasture. She knew that freak accidents had caused injuries in horses. Terrible things could happen with any kind of horse, but with a highly prized colt like Little Buddy...

She spent the next hour combing through the grass in the pastures, finding only a few branches and twigs. Both fields had already been pretty well tended. She was just finishing up her third tour around the lower pasture when Alec's pickup appeared in the driveway. Hurrying back to the barn, she found Billy and Alec talking by the water trough, their faces serious.

"What's up?" Danielle asked.

Alec crossed his arms over his chest. "It looks bad over at South Wind, Danielle. Moyer's filly made it through another night, but nothing short of a miracle is going to save her." He gave a helpless shrug and jerked his head toward the barn corridor. "So how's our colt?"

Danielle swallowed. "Fine," she said. "Real good." She couldn't help but think of the wish she'd made and how she might be responsible for the sick horses.

"Not a peep out of him," Billy added.

He and Alec started talking again, and Danielle wandered over to the house. Her conscience was really bothering her now about South Wind. How could she live with herself if anything happened to Mr. Moyer's filly or any of the other horses there? She felt guilty, all right, but what could she do?

Suddenly, she realized there *was* something she could do.

The horseshoe!

She still had one wish left: the one she was saving for Redman. If she accepted the fact that it would take her a long time to save money, she could use her last wish to ask for the horses at South Wind to get better. Nothing bad could come of that sort of wish, right? Maybe the horseshoe only worked for unselfish wishes. It was worth a try.

Danielle ran into the tool shed and rummaged

in the drawer where she thought she'd left the horseshoe.

It wasn't there.

Don't panic, she told herself. It had been over a week since she'd seen it. She couldn't remember exactly where and when she'd last had it. She quickly started opening and closing drawers, softly at first, then banging them in frustration.

The horseshoe was really gone! And so was her chance to make her last wish.

CHAPTER FOURTEEN

Lulu's Hideaway

Danielle racked her brains to remember where she'd left the horseshoe. But the harder she tried, the more confused she became. Where had she put the thing? *Wait a minute,* she told herself. She'd been looking at those funny markings on the horseshoe and put it down on the counter. She'd just left it there. And that was more than a week ago.

She gazed around the tool shed at all the piles of junk her brother had strewn about the place. Finding anything in this mess would be next to impossible. It would probably be better to wait until she could talk to Dylan and see if he might have any idea where her horseshoe was. Maybe it had gotten mixed up with the trash and thrown out by accident.

Giving up her search for the time being, Danielle headed back to the barn to see what needed doing there. Billy handed her some saddle soap and put her to work cleaning bridles while he did some paperwork, keeping one eye on the colt's stall. Little Buddy was sleeping for the moment.

After about twenty minutes of rubbing leather, Danielle blurted out, "Hey, Billy, you haven't seen a horseshoe lying around here anywhere, have you?"

"A horseshoe?" Billy seemed puzzled.

"A funny-looking little one, sort of a goldish color?"

The lanky cowboy looked up from his papers a moment and then back again. "Nope. No horseshoes around here that don't have horses connected to 'em."

"Are you sure?" Danielle pressed. "Maybe you picked it up by mistake?" As soon as the words were out of her mouth, she realized how silly they sounded.

Billy looked at her strangely. "What do you want this horseshoe for?"

"Oh, nothing. Never mind. It's just like, well, sort of a good luck charm."

"Hmmm." Billy pushed back his cowboy hat and scratched his head. "Sorry, Missy. Remind me and I'll bring you one from the farm, if you want."

Danielle shrugged. "Thanks, Billy. That's okay."

When Dylan came back from his can and bottle rounds, Danielle caught up to him in the tool shed. "Have you seen a horseshoe around anywhere?"

"Huh?" her brother said.

"A horseshoe, Dylan. I thought it was in here."

Dylan shook his head. "Why don't you just get one from Alec if you need it so badly?"

"Because this one was special," Danielle said.

"I'll look around, Danielle, but I really don't remember seeing any horseshoes. You're sure it was here?"

Danielle nodded emphatically. "I swear I left it on the counter. Or maybe in the drawer. But I just know it was around somewhere."

Dylan shrugged. "Take a look for yourself if you want."

"Are you kidding?" said Danielle, glaring at her brother. "Where am I supposed to start?" She picked up a cardboard box and dropped it, startled, when Lulu, Dylan's pet ferret, suddenly jumped out.

"There you are, Lu," her brother said as the big silver-colored ferret scurried across the room. He turned to Danielle. "Guess you found Lulu's latest hideout. They get lost in here sometimes, and I can't find them for days."

"Yeah," said Danielle, wrinkling her nose at the musky odor, "it smells like it." She started looking through boxes, moving them cautiously in case she stumbled on the other weasel's hide-out.

"There's an order to everything here," Dylan explained. He nodded toward a mound of junk piled against the wall at the far end of the tool shed.

"You've got your electrical-based household appliances over here. Vacuum cleaners, sewing machines and whatnot, except for the kitchen stuff, and..."

"That's okay, Dylan," Danielle broke in. "I get the picture."

She poked around the shelves over the desk but found no sign of her missing horseshoe. With a sigh, she gave up again and headed to the pastures.

The only good thing was that it was Friday, and there was no school on Monday because of some teachers' meeting. With the long weekend, at least she would have a few days to try to figure something out. But even if she found the horseshoe and made a wish to cure the horses at South Wind, would it really work? At least she could try. She *had* to.

Danielle spent an hour or so checking fence rails, then stopped back in the barn.

She watched Little Buddy, still cooped up in his stall. She was beginning to feel impatient, wondering why Alec was keeping the colt inside for so long.

Little Buddy nickered a greeting as Danielle stepped inside the stall. "What's up, Little Buddy?" she said. "You must be getting really bored." The colt nudged her pockets until Danielle pulled out a carrot, broke it in pieces, and fed them to him one at a time. She listened to the rhythmic chomping, gave the colt a good-night hug, then walked back outside.

Dylan had left to spend the weekend with friends in Daytona Beach, so Danielle headed to the tool shed to look for the ferrets. She'd promised to take care of them while he was away. Danielle always kidded her brother about his ferrets, how smelly they were and all, but deep down she liked them— even though they were about the nosiest little rascals she had ever met. They were always poking their noses into places they didn't belong.

She'd told Dylan that she would at least try to find them and put them back into their cage before she went to bed. But the chances of her finding the critters in that maze of junk were practically zero. "Lu...Tik..." she called. No answer.

Her brother had told her that his weasels were trained—well, semitrained—to come to the sound of a rubber squeaky toy. He always gave them a treat afterward. Danielle picked up the rubber duck and a handful of raisins from a shelf. Then she walked around the tool shed, squeaking the toy like crazy. A minute or two later, she heard scratching noises coming from a box in the corner. Reaching down, she put her hand inside. A touch of fur slipped from her grasp. Turning the box over, she uncovered the ferrets' latest stash: an old slipper, some radio parts, a half-eaten cookie, a gnawed-up chicken wing, a rubber drain stopper...

And her missing horseshoe.

Lulu and Tiki poked their raccoonlike faces over the edge of the box. The two of them gave Danielle an innocent "Who? Me?" look.

"You thieving little polecats," she scolded the furry-faced critters. She picked up the horseshoe and felt something sticky smearing her fingers. It took her a moment or two to figure out what it was—chicken grease. Gross. Danielle quickly wiped her hands on her jeans. That must have been why the ferrets were so interested in her horseshoe. She quickly put Lulu and Tiki in their cage. They sleepily climbed into their hammock and stretched out.

Now that she had found the horseshoe, the craziness of the whole situation began to trouble her once again. How could a horseshoe make wishes come true? But everything she'd wished for so far had come true. And this time, after making her wish, she was going to get rid of the thing.

It was definitely giving her the creeps. The sooner she got it over with, the better.

ᔓ CHAPTER FIFTEEN ᕫ

Last Wish

Danielle took the horseshoe outside and held it up to the sky. Then, trying to sound as solemn as she could, she said aloud:

"Merkain, thank you very much for letting me use your horseshoe, but now I would like you to take it back. For my final wish, please make the sick horses at South Wind get better and make the flu bug go away forever. I hope that counts as just one wish. Thanks again."

She walked back to the house and stuffed the horseshoe inside her knapsack so she wouldn't have to look at it. *Where can I get rid of this thing?* she wondered. She thought it over but couldn't come up with the perfect place. She wanted to make sure that no one ever found it again. She went into the living room and tried to distract herself by watching a movie on TV, but she fell asleep. Some time after midnight, her mom woke her up and told her to go to bed.

Perhaps it was the full moon that accounted for her dream, or maybe it was something she ate, but later that night Danielle had one of the worst nightmares of her entire life.

She dreamed she was walking in the woods above the upper pasture when she came to a clearing. A beautiful black horse was standing there, looking bold and fierce. He was fighting a tangled line that held him tied to a tree. She tried to untie the knot, but it was impossible.

Reaching into her jacket, she found a pocketknife and started opening blades, looking for something to cut the line. But this was a very strange pocketknife. She found a spoon, a fork, and nonsensical attachments like a miniature pepper grinder and a tiny oar. Finally, she located the right blade and cut the knot.

The stallion reared. Somehow, Danielle was suddenly on his back. He took off at a gallop, and the faster he ran, the tighter she held on. She couldn't jump off to save herself. He carried her down to the bottom of a lake, but still she wasn't able to get off. Then she felt herself helplessly sinking deeper and deeper into the water...

When Danielle woke up, her heart was racing a million miles an hour. She looked at the clock on her dresser. It was just before six in the morning.

She pulled on her jeans and a T-shirt, slung her knapsack over her shoulder, and headed to the barn to look in on Little Buddy. He was still asleep. It wasn't time for his breakfast yet, anyway. She walked outside again. The fresh air quickly cleared her head of the lingering terror left by her nightmare.

Why had she had such an awful dream? Then she remembered the story she'd read in the library about the Kelpie horses who took their riders to the bottom of the sea. It must have affected her more than she'd realized.

Maybe the horseshoe hadn't had anything to do with her nightmare, Danielle thought. Then again, maybe it did. Either way, the time had come to get rid of the thing for good. She wasn't going to wait another minute. She hopped onto her bike and pedaled into the dawn, following the road by the interstate. When she reached the tree that had been struck by lightning she stopped. She could just put the horseshoe back where she found it. *No,* she decided, that didn't feel right.

Then she noticed a small pond in a field about fifty yards from the tree. Perfect. She squirmed under a barbed-wire fence and walked to the edge of the pond. Removing the horseshoe from her bag, she took a deep breath and gave it one last rub for luck. All three of the horseshoe's stars were green now, as if to signal that all the wishes were spent. That seemed like a good sign, Danielle thought. She remembered her last wish, the one to help the sick horses at South Wind, and wondered if it really would come true. She hoped so.

She closed her eyes and threw the horseshoe as hard as she could out over the middle of the pond. With a splash, it was gone. Not daring to look back, she turned and ran to the road. A heavy weight seemed to have been lifted from her shoulders. She quickly jumped on her bike and rode home.

Danielle spent most of the morning with the lonesome little colt, reading to him from her book and talking to him the way she used to do with Redman. "I can't understand why Alec is keeping you locked up in here like this," she said as the colt paced back and forth in front of the stall door. "I mean, I can see it for a day or two, but this doesn't make any sense."

The colt gazed pitifully at Danielle. "Don't give me those sad eyes, Little Buddy," she said. "You know Alec would kill me if I let you out of there. His orders haven't changed at all from day one. There's nothing I can do except try to make you comfortable." The colt bobbed his head and turned his attention back to the door. He seemed to have surrendered. There was very little desperate whinnying now.

When Danielle returned to the barn after lunch,

Little Buddy began showing interest in her pocket. She pulled out a piece of carrot and held it out to him. She felt his warm, damp breath on her fingers. A second later, the soft muzzle touched her hand. She held it still and steady as the colt ate. When he was finished, she ran her hands over his fine black coat and down along his legs, talking softly. "You've been such a good boy, Buddy," she said. "I'll make it up to you once we get you out of here. We're going to have all sorts of fun, I promise."

She took him by the halter and attempted to lead him to the corner feed box and hay rack. The colt refused, his eyes becoming frightened again. He turned his head to the door, neighed a few times, then turned back to Danielle and licked the palm of her hand. Danielle held still and then took hold of his halter again. This time the colt followed her to the feed box.

"Well, well," came a voice from outside the stall. Alec had slipped into the barn unnoticed. "Looks like he's ready for the pasture tomorrow."

Danielle smiled. "Great," she said. The end of prison for the colt at last!

The next morning, Alec and Danielle turned Little Buddy loose. Danielle and the colt chased each other around the pasture until Danielle was too tired to keep up. She lay down on the grass under a tree and caught her breath. A shift in the wind direction made her glance up to the sky. An army of dark clouds was gathering in the western sky. Rather than take the chance of getting caught out in another storm, Danielle brought little Buddy inside right away. Using the lead line, she tied him in the corridor for a few minutes to get him used to standing tied. Alec walked over and gave the colt a pat.

"All the work you've been doing with him is paying off, Danielle," Alec said. "You're making it real easy for me with Little Buddy. He'll be ready for bridle and saddle soon."

Danielle's eyes shone with pride. "Really?"

"Sure," Alec said. "But no rush. We need to have a lot of patience." Danielle nodded.

Mrs. Conners suddenly appeared at the barn door, dressed in a peach-colored suit. "Danielle?" she called.

"In here, Mom," Danielle answered. Alec and Mrs. Conners exchanged hellos. Then Mrs. Conners turned to her daughter and dug a letter out of her purse.

"This came in the mail on Saturday. It got mixed up with some bills, so I just found it now."

Danielle looked at the envelope. "It's from Mr. Sweet!" she said, grabbing the letter in both hands.

Mrs. Conners gave Danielle an understanding smile, then glanced anxiously toward the barn door.

"You can tell me about it later," she said, excusing herself. "I'm late for an appointment at the bank."

"Thanks, Mom," Danielle called after her. "I've been expecting this."

"I know. See you," she said, leaving the barn.

"That letter's from the guy who bought Redman?" Alec asked.

"Sure is," Danielle said. "Want to hear what it says?"

"Okay," Alec replied. "If that's all right with you." He knew what getting Redman back meant to her.

Danielle ripped the letter open and started reading aloud. "'Dear Ms. Conners, In answer to your recent inquiry concerning Redman, please be assured that he is in good hands and is being well cared for. Reports from the manager of the camp have been very positive regarding all of the horses we sent up, including yours. Also, I'd like to take this opportunity to officially confirm our agreement regarding the Redman matter. Providing a replacement horse can be found, I will sell Redman back, as long as you have earned the money yourself.'"

Danielle stopped reading and waved the letter in the air. "There it is!" she said excitedly. "Now it's official, in black and white. Redman can come home."

Alec smiled. "That's great," he said softly. Danielle turned back to the letter.

"Let's see," she said, scanning down to the bottom of the page, "then he says...Ha! Get this. He ends by complimenting me on my handwriting and correct spelling." Danielle silently congratulated herself on not being too lazy to use a dictionary. She kissed the letter, then carefully folded it up and tucked it in her pocket.

Just then, Billy ran into the barn. "Hey, Alec," he said. "Good news."

Danielle and Alec looked at each other. "More good news?" Danielle asked. "First Buddy, then Redman, now what?"

Alec smiled. "I sure do like these kind of winning streaks."

Billy actually smiled under his droopy mustache. "I was just over to South Wind," he said. "Those sick horses are on the mend." Danielle's mouth dropped open. "Even Moyer's filly seems to have turned a corner. The vet thinks she should pull through, after all. He has no idea what happened. He thinks one of the new anti-flu drugs he tried must have worked."

"Or maybe the bug just ran its course. Either way, that's really great news, Billy." Alec said.

Or maybe it was my wish, Danielle thought.

"Whatever doesn't kill 'em makes 'em stronger, I guess," Billy said.

"What do you mean?" Danielle asked, curious.

For once Billy didn't seem to mind answering

her question. "It's like this, kid," he said. "Having survived the flu has left those horses better off than before. It helped them develop their own antibodies to the germs that caused the epidemic."

Alec nodded. "Next time—if there *is* a next time—maybe they won't get sick," he explained.

Danielle smiled to herself. Her final wish had come true, all right. Whether it was just one last coincidence didn't matter. *Let the vets take credit for saving the horses,* Danielle thought. *The important thing is that the horses recovered.*

To celebrate, Alec ran into the Coop and brought out Cokes for the three of them. They talked and joked and kidded around, feeling like a team that had just won a game.

Suddenly, Danielle grew quiet. She left Alec and Billy, took her soda, and walked over to check on Little Buddy. Now that the epidemic seemed to be over, would Alec move him back to South Wind? she wondered. And what about Redman? She was still hundreds of dollars short of her goal of earning enough money to bring him home. Without a job, she'd be stuck right back where she'd been before, picking up cans and bottles. It was great that the sick horses at South Wind were getting better, but...

Her eyes wandered over to Redman's empty stall. *Did I really give up a chance to bring him home?* she asked herself. *Why did I waste that first wish on a stupid linguini dinner, one I practically didn't eat?* It made her mad just to think about it.

Oh well, she thought, There's nothing I can do about it now. And deep down, she knew she'd done the right thing using her last wish to help the South Wind horses.

She walked back to the tack room, where Alec and Billy were still talking. *Should I ask Alec about Little Buddy?* she thought. She might as well find out any bad news now.

She waited for a lull in the conversation and then turned to Alec. "So if everything's okay at South Wind," she said, "does that mean Buddy will be going back there soon?"

Danielle could tell by the look in Alec's eyes that the answer to her question was probably yes. She also guessed that he didn't want to spoil this celebration by telling her so. "We'll see, Danielle," he said finally. "I'll talk to Henry about it. In the meantime "

Danielle sighed. "I know, I know. Let's enjoy the good news while it lasts." She held up her Coke can for a toast. "Here's to healthy, happy horses." Alec and Billy joined her, lifting their sodas. "Hear, hear," they said together.

When Danielle came home from school the next day, Little Buddy was prancing around the pasture. She spent the whole afternoon with him.

After dinner, her mom began rearranging kitchen shelves. Climbing up on a chair to reach the top cupboard, she started screwing in cup hooks to make more room.

"Danielle," Mrs. Conners called as she balanced on her chair, "Do me a favor, will you? Go out to the tool shed and bring me a pair of pliers."

"Sure, Mom," Danielle said.

Inside the tool shed, she snapped on the light and began rummaging around in the tool drawer. The pliers weren't in the box where they were usually kept. Suddenly, she saw something in the bottom drawer that wasn't supposed to be there.

The horseshoe.

CHAPTER SIXTEEN

Secret in the Stars

Danielle turned and ran from the tool shed as if her clothes were on fire. The next thing she knew, she was upstairs in her room catching her breath behind a locked door.

How can the horseshoe be in a drawer in the tool shed when I tossed it into a pond? she asked herself. It didn't make sense. And the thought of a horseshoe moving around on its own, disappearing and reappearing in different places, scared her to death. Maybe the ferrets really hadn't taken the horseshoe before. Maybe...

"Danielle?" her mom called from the other side of the door.

Danielle quickly opened some schoolbooks on her desk, trying to look busy. Mrs. Conners knocked, then tried the doorknob. "Hey, why is the door locked? What are you doing in there? Danielle!" She rattled the knob again.

Danielle got up and opened the door. "Sorry, Mom."

"And what's the big idea of leaving me stranded in the kitchen? I thought you went to get me some pliers.

"I couldn't find them. Then I sort of...forgot."

Mrs. Conners gave her daughter a concerned look. "Danielle, are you all right?"

"Sure, it's nothing, Mom. Sorry about the pliers."

Danielle's mom glanced around the room and noticed the schoolbooks open on the desk. She shrugged. "Well, that's okay. I managed without them." She gave Danielle a pat on the shoulders. "Sometimes I worry about you, honey, that's all."

"I'm okay, Mom, really."

Mrs. Conners nodded slowly. "I have to say, though, you look as if you've just seen a ghost." Danielle forced a smile. Her mom had no idea how right she was. "I'll let you get back to your homework, or whatever it is you're doing up here," Mrs. Conners said. "Leave the door unlocked, will you?"

"Sure, Mom," Danielle said.

After her mom left, Danielle leaned against the door, still shaking. How could the horseshoe have reappeared like that? Had she been seeing things? Or sleepwalking somehow? No. She'd touched it, she remembered. The horseshoe was real.

Her thoughts raced. What if she couldn't *ever* get rid of the thing? What if it haunted her forever, along with the nightmare about endless rides on a midnight stallion?

Stop it! Danielle ordered herself. *This is crazy.* Maybe in the morning she'd find she was mistaken about the horseshoe coming back. She'd look again, in broad daylight. And there was nothing else she could do right now. There was no way she was going back out to that tool shed now.

She tossed and turned all night. Once again, her dreams were filled with wild images of tearing through the countryside on a runaway stallion, racing headlong into cold, dark water.

After finishing her morning chores and a quick breakfast, Danielle returned to the tool shed. Holding her breath, she slowly opened the drawer. The horseshoe was still there. Danielle gasped and slammed the drawer shut. Then she grabbed her bike and pedaled to the bus stop as fast as she could.

Somehow, Danielle got through her first-period math class. As she stepped out into the hallway, Julie ran up and pulled her over against a bank of lockers.

"He's here!" she said, breathlessly.

Danielle frowned. "Who's here?"

"Mr. Lyman! I saw him coming out of the teachers lounge. He must be subbing today."

I can tell him about Merkain's horseshoe! Danielle thought excitedly. "Wait a minute," she said. "Didn't he go up north?"

"Well, if he did, he's back." Julie glanced down the hallway. "It must be another one of your weird coincidences. Hey, there he goes. You'd better catch him before the bell rings. Good luck."

Danielle dashed off. As she turned the corner, she saw Mr. Lyman walking into his classroom. Finally, someone who might be able to understand what was happening to her and explain everything! She hurried after him.

Mr. Lyman agreed to give Danielle a few moments and listened carefully to her story. He didn't laugh when she finished speaking, but his face slowly broke into a smile. "Danielle," he said, smoothing back the dark hair on his temples, "I don't know exactly what you found out by the road the other day, but one thing I do know. It wasn't Merkain's horseshoe. The story I told your class last month was, I'm afraid, just a story. I made it up. I was putting on a show for you guys—that's all."

"You *what?*" Danielle gasped. Mr. Lyman had lied to them! "You mean that wasn't a real Celtic myth? But what about the Kelpies? You didn't make them up. I read about them in a library book."

"There are elements of truth in every fictional story, Danielle," Mr. Lyman said. "Besides being a teacher, I'm a storyteller. A writer. I like to try out things I'm working on with new listeners."

"So you mean that none of that stuff about Merkain was true? You were just using our class as a test audience?" Danielle really felt stupid now.

Mr. Lyman smiled again. "Well, sort of. The story was based on a folktale I heard when I was a graduate student traveling in Ireland. Merkain is definitely a figure in Irish legend. And there are stories of people using horseshoes as talismans, which are charmed objects, for lack of a better definition. But I did put the two ideas together. As far as Merkain having a horseshoe, well, I made that up."

The bell rang. "I'm sorry, Danielle," Mr. Lyman said. "I didn't realize you'd taken the story so seriously. I never intended—"

"That's okay," Danielle said, flushing with embarrassment. "I guess my imagination got carried away, too."

Mr Lyman shrugged. "Who knows, Danielle? Maybe you *did* find something really special. Stranger things have happened in this world than wishes coming true."

"I suppose so," Danielle said slowly. Then she smiled in spite of herself.

"I'd be interested in seeing that horseshoe of yours sometime. Why don't you bring it to school to show everyone." He glanced at his watch as students began streaming into the classroom. "You'd better get going, I think. Bye now."

Danielle thanked the teacher and hustled down the hall to her next class. So Merkain's horseshoe had been only a story. Boy, did she feel dumb. But something else was nagging at the back of her mind. How had that horseshoe gotten back into the tool drawer after she threw it into the lake?

The rest of the school day went by in a haze. Either she'd been dreaming when she tossed the horseshoe in the lake or...what? The horseshoe hadn't just swum over to the bank, walked back to her house, and climbed into the drawer all on its own. Certainly, no one had retrieved it. And this time she couldn't blame Dylan's ferrets, either.

It simply didn't make sense. She thought about what Mr. Lyman had told her. Maybe the horseshoe she'd found didn't belong to Merkain. But there was definitely something strange about it.

Back at the house after school, Danielle went straight to the tool shed. Dylan was there, fixing his bike. He had the radio up full blast, playing some heavy metal band. She ignored him and went straight to the workbench and the bottom drawer. Taking a deep breath, she opened it up and pulled out the horseshoe.

It was her horseshoe, all right. There was the same funny writing, the same stars. *Wait a minute,*

Danielle thought. They *were* different. The stars had turned gold again!

Did this mean she had three more wishes?

Dylan turned down the radio. "So I guess you found it," he said.

"Yeah," Danielle said, a little shakily. "More like *it* found *me.*"

Dylan shrugged. "Well, Merry Christmas, anyway."

Danielle frowned. "What are you talking about, Dylan? Christmas is more than a month away."

"Well, that horseshoe was going to be your present, sister dear. Isn't it just like that one you lost and went so nuts about? I got it in Daytona at a garage sale."

Danielle gazed down at the horseshoe. It *did* look exactly the same as the other one. And she'd never told her brother about finding the horseshoe in the ferrets' stash.

"It's some sort of Chinese door knocker," Dylan went on. "That's what the man who sold it to me said, anyway. Maybe you'll find the one you lost and make a set. Pretty cool, huh?"

Danielle turned the horseshoe over in her hand. "So the writing is Chinese?"

"Guess so," Dylan said, shrugging. "The guy said it translates as 'Good luck' or something." He put down his screwdriver. "I liked the worn-out look your other one had, though. The oxidation made it look really cool."

"Oxidation?"

"Yeah, all that greenish stuff. Corrosion. You know how brass turns green when it gets wet?"

So that's why the stars turned green, Danielle thought. They must have been made of brass and changed color with the wet weather. Come to think of it, she realized now, every time she'd made a wish it had just rained, or was about to.

Danielle decided not to tell her brother the whole story. She might never hear the end of it if she did. She turned to leave.

"Hey, aren't you going to take your present?" Dylan called after her.

Danielle grinned. "It's a cool gift, Dylan. Thanks. Save it for Christmas, though. I can wait that long."

Danielle looked outside. It was beginning to rain. She thought about Redman. Well, she could still wish for her horse to come home. What was it Mr. Lyman had said?

Stranger things have happened in this world than wishes coming true.

Team Raven

Danielle dashed through the rain to the barn. She found Alec there, standing outside Little Buddy's stall. He was holding a large white envelope. "Hey, Danielle. Take a look at this."

"What is it?" Danielle asked.

"Buddy's papers."

The colt was nosing around in the hay rack. They left him in his stall and Danielle followed Alec into the tack room. Opening the envelope, he withdrew a long application blank. "We're going to register the colt with the Association so we can race him," Alec said. He sat down and took up a pen from the desk.

Peering over Alec's shoulder, Danielle saw the outline drawings of a horse's profile, body, and head. "This is where we point out any of the colt's identifying marks—stockings, blaze, stars, that sort of thing," Alec explained. He marked the "star" and drew one in the outline of the horse's forehead. The line below read "color." Alec wrote "black."

"Not dark brown?" Danielle asked.

"Nope," Alec said, shaking his head. "It's one of the strangest things I've ever seen. You remember how he looked when we first brought him here."

Danielle nodded. "His coat was a dark, dark brown, but not quite black."

"Well, look at him now," Alec said. "He's grown even darker over the last few weeks. Usually they get lighter, if anything. I don't think we can call him anything but black."

Alec circled "horse" in the column headed "horse, gelding, mare." He skipped "name selected," and glanced at Danielle. "Any ideas?"

"Me?" Danielle raised her eyebrows. "Um, no, sorry. Why are we doing all this now when Little Buddy's racing days are such a long way off?" she asked.

"Well, for one thing, the later you wait to register a foal, the more it costs," Alec answered.

"So he'll be considered a yearling after January first?"

Alec nodded. "That's right, even though he'll really be only a little more than seven months old. Horses born earlier in the year will have a few months on him and still be called yearlings like him. That can make a difference when they start racing and all go to the post as two-year-olds."

The sudden sound of neighing trumpeted down the barn corridor. Alec quickly got up and went to check on the colt. Danielle looked over the registration papers spread out on the desk. *This is it,* she thought. *Little Buddy is really growing up.*

How long could it be before he was moved back to South Wind?

Alec came back to the tack room a minute later. "Buddy's okay," Alec said. "He just wants to remind us he's here, I guess."

After finishing the last line of the application, Alec put the pen down and turned to Danielle. "So okay, I'm serious now. Do you have any thoughts about a name for this guy? We can't keep calling him Little Buddy for the rest of his life."

"How about just plain Buddy then?"

Alec looked at her and Danielle could tell he wasn't crazy about that idea. "No, I mean it, Danielle. Come on, think. Something that fits him."

"Well, the Black is his sire," Danielle said slowly. "We could call him Black something or other."

Alec shook his head. "I'd rather it was just one name instead of two. Something short and easy to remember."

Danielle and Alec threw names around for a few minutes, but none of them felt right. Finally, Alec got up from his chair.

"I have to get into town to meet Billy," he said. "You're in charge of the colt until I get back, okay?"

Danielle nodded.

"I need to mail in this application first thing in the morning. We definitely need a name by then."

"I'll think of one, Alec," Danielle said, "I promise."

After Alec left, Little Buddy was quiet for a while, so Danielle looked around the barn for something to do to keep her busy. Maybe it would help her think. She started straightening up the tack room, even though it really didn't need it, mulling over names as she worked. She went back to check on the colt, who was leaning his head out over the half door of his stall. She put one hand on Little Buddy's neck and stroked his face with the other. Then she just stood there awhile, holding him and thinking.

"See what happens when you grow up?" Danielle told him, "how complicated everything gets? But I guess Alec's right. We can't keep calling you Little Buddy forever. You're just too darn big now." The colt flicked his ears and bobbed his head in reply.

With a sigh, Danielle sat down on the tack trunk outside his stall. She picked up the pen and started scribbling names on a pad of paper. Before she knew it, she was lost in thought again and staring out the window at the back of Buddy's stall.

It had stopped raining, and doves were darting

between the treetops. She gazed after them, and a picture of the colt came to her mind. Sometimes the way he ran was so graceful, as though he was just gliding along over the grass...

Or flying...

Merkain? *No way*, Danielle told herself, shuddering.

A bird name, maybe? The full name of the colt's mother was Prima Gavilan. Hadn't Alec told her that Gavilan was Spanish for falcon or hawk?

Black Hawk? No, that was too long. But it was close. Buddy's brother's name was Black Falcon, after all. Danielle tried to think of a big black bird in full flight. The only black birds around Wishing Wells were crows, or bats, but they didn't even count as birds.

Black Bat? Danielle smiled at herself. *Right.* Maybe a vampire name.

Dracula? Black Drac. Ugh.

Wait a minute, Danielle thought suddenly. What was the name of that Edgar Allan Poe poem they'd read in school? The one about that spooky black bird?

The Raven.

That might work. Danielle printed the name on her notepad. It sounded good. A little scary maybe, but in a nice way.

The familiar red pickup truck pulled into the

muddy driveway and stopped. Alec and Billy got out and came into the barn. Alec glanced at the notepad on Danielle's knee. "So how's it going with the name game?" he asked.

"Okay, how about this, you guys," Danielle said excitedly. Think of a big black bird flying through the moonlit sky..."

Alec stopped her. "Raven," he said immediately.

Danielle nodded.

Billy frowned. "Too touchy-feely for me. I could see a falcon or hawk. Or an eagle, maybe."

Danielle ran into the tack room and picked up a dictionary from the desk. She looked up definitions of the word "raven," then hurried back to show the others what she'd found. "Listen to this," she said, reading aloud. "'A glossy black bird, also the glossy sheen of the raven.' And then there's this one, 'to rush, to take by force.'"

Billy nodded. "That's a lot better."

"This colt's gonna be fast, all right," Alec said.

"Faster than any scraggly old bird," Billy added.

"Well, how about this?" Danielle continued. "'To devour...to feed hungrily...to prowl for food...to prey...to plunder.' That doesn't sound so soft and cuddly to me."

"Sounds good," Alec said finally. He looked at Billy. "Agreed?"

Billy shrugged.

"Come on, Billy," pleaded Danielle gently. "We could be Team Raven."

Billy hesitated a moment or two. Then his face broke into a smile. "Team Raven, huh? I'm just yanking your chain, missy. Raven's a fine name. It suits him, all right."

"Raven it is," Alec said. He picked up the registration papers and started to write.

"Great," Danielle said, feeling proud.

"By the way, it looks like this farm is going to be Raven's nest for a while longer," Alec said, without looking up. "I just talked with Henry on the phone. He said that since the colt seemed to be doing so well here, we should hold off on sending him back to South Wind. For the time being, anyway."

"Henry said that?" Danielle asked.

"Yeah, it surprised me, too," Alec said, shaking his head. "Who knows? Maybe some of that laid-back California lifestyle is rubbing off on him."

"That's so cool!" Danielle said eagerly. "Now I can keep making money to bring Redman home, too."

"Well, there's going to be plenty of work to do around here, that's for sure," Alec said. "Are you up for it, Danielle?

"You bet!"

Danielle opened the colt's stall door and stepped inside. The little horse was sniffing the corners of his feed box, cleaning up the last bit of oats. Danielle stroked his neck.

"So how about it, guy?" she said. "Does 'Raven' sound okay to you, Little...I mean, Mr. Raven?"

Raven bobbed his head in approval. He stretched his long, supple neck to the rack above him and quietly munched his hay. There was no more desperate neighing, no more lonesome pining for his mother.

Danielle smiled. At long last, the colt named Raven was learning to be on his own. And so was she. Together, with Alec and Billy's help, they were going to make it.

They were Team Raven.

About the Author

Steven Farley is the son of the late Walter Farley, the man who started the tradition with the best-loved horse story of all time, *The Black Stallion*.

A freelance writer based in Manhattan, Steven Farley travels frequently, especially to places where he can enjoy riding, diving, and surfing. Along with the *Young Black Stallion* series, Mr. Farley has written *The Black Stallion's Shadow*, *The Black Stallion's Steeplechaser*, and *The Young Black Stallion*, a collaborative effort with his father.